PRINCE VALIANT

Special thanks to the SPECIAL COLLECTIONS RESEARCH CENTER of the SYRACUSE UNIVERSITY LIBRARY for providing the scans for the vast majority of the *Prince Valiant* strips, reproduced from original syndicate proof sheets, in this volume. Visit their website at http://library.syr.edu/find/scrc/

Prince Valiant Vol. 14: 1963–1964 Fantagraphics Books, Inc. 7563 Lake City Way NE, Seattle, WA 98115. Edited by Brian M. Kane. Editorial Liaison: Gary Groth. Series design by Adam Grano. Production by Michael Heck. Restoration by Paul Baresh. Associate Publisher: Eric Reynolds. Publisher: Gary Groth. All comics © 2015 King Features Syndicate. Introduction ©2016 Roger Stern. "Land and Sea: Hal Foster's Fine Art Paintings" copyright © 2016 Brian Kane. This edition copyright © 2016 Fantagraphics Books, Inc. All rights reserved. Permission to quote or reproduce material for reviews or notices must be obtained from Fantagraphics Books, in writing, at 7563 Lake City Way NE, Seattle, WA 98115. First edition: June 2016 ISBN: 978-1-60699-970-7. Library of Congress Control Number: 2016946604. Printed in China.

PRINCE VALIANT

VOL. 14: 1963-1964 — BY HAL FOSTER

PUBLISHED BY FANTAGRAPHICS BOOKS, INC., SEATTLE.

Top row: *Samples of Hal Foster's 1928* Tarzan of the Apes *comic strip used in the creation of Batman's origin in* Detective Comics #31 *(1939).*

Second row: *Jack Kirby's* The Demon *(1971) was based on a 1937* Prince Valiant *story.*

Third row: *A 1938* Prince Valiant *panel compared to Shelly Moldoff's swipe for a "Hawkman" story in* Flash #7 *(1940).*

Bottom row: *A 1937 Prince Valiant panel as reinterpreted by Frank Frazetta (*Thun'da, *1952), Everett Raymond Kinstler (*Strange Worlds *# 6, 1952), and Fernando (*Psycho *#11, 1973).*

SWIPING MR. FOSTER:
A LEGACY IN FOUR COLORS

Foreword by Roger Stern

Back in the late 1960s, young fan artists who aspired to work in the comic book industry had a lot of role models. They wanted to draw like Jack Kirby or Steve Ditko, like Gil Kane or Joe Kubert, like John Buscema or John Romita. But if and when you got the chance to speak with those gentlemen, you soon learned that the artists they themselves idolized were Milton Caniff, Alex Raymond, and Hal Foster.

Caniff, Raymond, and Foster. To the professional artists, they were like a holy trinity of comics art. Noted writer, artist, and historian Jim Steranko has called them "the triumvirate that spawned the overwhelming multitude of four-color draftsmen—even Kirby! They are the trunk of the comicbook tree; everyone else is a branch, a twig, or a leaf."[1] To some of us young fan whippersnappers, it could be a bit confusing. Sure, Caniff's *Steve Canyon* was still appearing in plenty of newspapers, but many of us had never seen his earlier work on *Terry and the Pirates.* Raymond had died in 1956, and we didn't know that he'd drawn *Flash Gordon.* Back before there was an Internet, there was no easy way to access an artist's past works. Most of us wouldn't see Raymond's *Gordon* until Nostalgia Press began reprinting it in hardcover editions.

And Foster?

Well, some of us were lucky enough to live in areas where *Prince Valiant* appeared in the Sunday papers, but many of us were not. And even if your local newspaper did carry *Valiant,* it didn't necessarily present the series in all its glory.

For example, where I grew up in the Midwest, *Prince Valiant* was chopped and channeled to a mere third of a Sunday newspaper page. I'm sure that was one of the reasons why, as a callow youth, I didn't quite understand the series.[2] I mean, I could tell that *Prince Valiant* was well-drawn, but it always looked a little dark and murky to me. I had no idea how much that was a consequence of the lousy printing that the cut-down version was getting in the *Indianapolis Star.*

It wasn't until I was in college that I saw a high-quality reproduction of a full broadsheet-page *Prince Valiant.* That page was breathtaking. The colors, the detail! Clearly, it was a work of art. Plus, at full size, it was a lot easier to follow—and read—the story.

Then and there, I started to get it. I finally understood why the comics artists, whose work I admired, ranked Foster along with Caniff and Raymond in their big three.

Some even liked their work to the point of copying it. Or, in the language of the professional artist, "swiping it."

Swiping, in the words of author/cartoonist Jules Feiffer, "was and is a trade term in comic books for appropriating that which is Alex Raymond's, Milton Caniff's, Hal Foster's, or anyone of a number of other sources and making it one's own."[3] It's a practice that sometimes raises the hackles of readers—and other artists—leading to accusations of plagiarism. On the other hand, fine-art students have, for centuries, honed their craft by copying old masters. Commercial artists routinely kept files of photographs and drawings to swipe for their work. Early comic book publishers and editors would sometimes turn a blind eye to their young artists' swipes … and other times outright encourage them to emulate the newspaper cartoonists.

That emulation ran the gamut, everything from trying to capture a style to virtual tracing.

"We were competing with the newspapers," recalled Golden Age artist Sheldon "Shelly" Moldoff. "When [the publisher] picked up the Sunday papers, he saw *Flash Gordon, Prince Valiant, Terry and the Pirates.* We all leaned on these guys to learn—and we were very lucky, because while we were learning, we were selling the product …"[4]

We may never know how many comic book panels were inspired by—or copied from—Foster's work, but a few of the more obvious

swipes have gained notice in recent years. And the artists behind those swipes include some of the better known names in comics—people like, say, Bob Kane.

Robert Kane had gotten his start in comic books in the late 1930s, drawing humor strips such as *Peter Pupp* and *Ginger Snap,* before trying his hand at the more adventurous fare of *Rusty and his Pals* and *Clip Carson.* Of course, Kane is best known for creating DC Comics' *Batman,* along with the then-uncredited writer Bill Finger. In recent years, much has been made of Kane's early swipes of Alex Raymond and illustrator Henry E. Vallely, but he also copied at least one pose from Hal Foster.

In this case, Kane copied a classic pose of Foster's Tarzan from the 1928 newspaper strip, turning the jungle hero into the Batman for *Detective Comics* #31.[5] Kane must have really liked that swipe, as he used it again in *Detective Comics* #33,[6] and again in *Detective Comics* #34.[7]

Interestingly, Dell Publishing's *Large Feature Comic* #5, which reprinted that *Tarzan* panel, had gone on sale about a week before *Detective Comics* #33. One wonders if young readers of the time noticed the similarity of the two heroes' poses.

Sheldon "Shelly" Moldoff was a versatile artist who got his start producing filler pages for DC, with one of his earliest drawings appearing in *Action Comics* #1. He soon became one of Bob Kane's many ghost artists, and is believed to have worked on the aforementioned issues of *Detective Comics.* And Moldoff's artwork was soon turning up—credited under his own

A panel from Hal Foster's 1928, Tarzan of the Apes *compared to Frank Frazetta's paperback book cover for* Tarzan and the Lost Empire.

Top left: *A 1938* Prince Valiant *panel and Joe Simon's cover to* Red Raven #1 (1940).

Top right: *Foster's 1928* Tarzan of the Apes *and a page from Frazetta's sketchbook.*

Middle left: *Foster's* Tarzan *from March 1934, compared to a June 1934* Flash Gordon *panel by Alex Raymond.*

Middle right and bottom: *Many panels in Moldoff's "The Black Pirate" story in* Action Comics #42, 1941 *were swiped from various* Prince Valiant *strips dated 1940 & 1941.*

byline this time—on the *Hawkman* strip in *Flash Comics*, and on the *Black Pirate* series, which he created for *Action Comics* in 1940.

"Alex Raymond's *Flash Gordon* and Hal Foster's *Prince Valiant* became the style for adventure strips, which many of us younger artists tried to emulate," Moldoff admitted in later years. "I was criticized for copying Raymond, but I was trying to make it as good as possible to win readers, to make them appreciate comic books."[8]

And win readers, he did. Decades after it first saw print, Jules Feiffer remembered Shelly's work fondly, writing, "*Hawkman*, a special favorite of mine, gave an aged and blended look to its swipes—a sheen so formidable, I often preferred the swipe to the original …"[9]

On *Hawkman*, Moldoff mainly relied upon Raymond for inspiration—his Carter Hall and Shiera Sanders often resembled Flash Gordon and Dale Arden—but the occasional Foster swipes snuck into the work. On just his second outing on the *Hawkman* series, Shelly borrowed figures and scenes from four separate *Prince Valiant* panels.[10] Moldoff also borrowed poses and faces for the *Hawkman* story two issues later,[11] and incorporated a few more Foster swipes in his *Black Pirate* series.[12]

Jack Kirby was in his early twenties when he and Joe Simon created Captain America, and he didn't stop there. Along with Simon, he created the romance comics genre, and he had a hand in just about every other type of comic, from funny animals to Westerns. With Stan Lee, Kirby created the Fantastic Four, Ant-Man and the Wasp, the Hulk, Thor, the Avengers, the X-Men, the Black Panther, and the Silver Surfer. On his own, he created the Forever People, the New Gods, Mister Miracle, Kamandi, and the Demon. Jack has so many credits—as both an artist and a writer—that they would easily fill these pages. Kirby has been an inspiration to generations of comic book professionals, and his creations continue to

Top: *"Chad" Grothkopf's character "The Ancient One" in* Action Comics *#36, 1941, is a direct descendant of the "Giant" from* Prince Valiant *1940.*

Bottom: *In 1992, Don Rosa's "The Last of the Clan McDuck" story featured architectural similarities to a castle in* Prince Valiant *(from 1942).*

provide source material for the comics, as well as for the motion picture industry.

Genius is not too strong a title for Jack Kirby, but even he was inspired by others. "I loved the newspaper strips," Kirby remembered. "The comics are so large and colorful. The pages are extremely large, and I used to love that. And *Prince Valiant*, of course, it was astonishing to see this beautiful illustration in the newspaper, and it was so different from the ordinary comic."[13]

"Here's the reality: Even Kirby swiped images created by other artists," wrote Steranko. "Jack had loads of pulps and books he referenced."[14]

At Timely, the company that would later become Marvel Comics, Kirby witnessed artists swiping Foster. One such swipe appears on the cover of *Red Raven Comics* #1, illustrated by Joe Simon, Kirby's long-time partner.[15] Simon dynamically portrayed the title character, swooping in to save the day, but there's an element of the cover—one of the villains of the piece—that seems out of place, as if drawn by someone else. A second look shows why: the strange figure on the castle rampart is swiped from Foster's *Prince Valiant* for January 15, 1938.[16] It's a minor swipe, as things go, barely a footnote, but it set a precedent.

Thirty years later, Kirby would more deliberately use Foster as a source. Author and Kirby historian Mark Evanier remembers Kirby paging through a book of early *Prince Valiant* strips, "until he found a sequence he recalled, wherein Valiant disguised himself by stretching a goose skin over his head, thereby creating a grotesque mask—a memorable visual that Jack (and many readers of the strip) had recalled for decades. Jack thought it would serve as an inside joke for readers who recognized the source if he patterned the look of [his latest] character after that mask."[17]

Thus did Hal Foster's *Prince Valiant* for December 25, 1937, provide the visual inspiration, in 1971, for the face of Jack Kirby's The Demon.

Charles "Chad" Grothkopf was a pioneer of animation for television, having created the eight-minute short *Willie the Worm*, which NBC aired—way back in 1938!—for the handful of primitive radio-television receivers that then existed in the New York City area.[18] He is best known among comics fans of a certain age as the artist/creator of *Hoppy the Marvel Bunny*—the rabbit doppelgänger of Fawcett Comics' Captain Marvel—and as the artist of the *Howdy Doody* newspaper comic strip. But before his involvement in comics of the funny variety, Chad worked on a number of adventure strips during the Golden Age of Comics.

"I always tell people it was 'hunger' that got me into the business. I started out at Detective Comics (DC Comics) in 1938," Grothkopf recalled. "That was a great time there because they were just starting out. We got seven bucks a page for writing, drawing and lettering. It was a chance to show off our work for those of us

THEY SEARCH THE CITY IN DARKNESS, FOR NO TORCH WILL STAY ALIGHT IN THIS STORM. NOR IS VAL AND HIS PRISONER IN THE CITY.
410 12-17-44

7. HEFT 30 PFG.

Hartmuth
der junge Held

In Bodowars Gewalt!

⑤

AND THE YOUNG PRINCE IS ABLE TO LIBERATE ILENE'S FATHER, THE THANE OF BRANWYN, WHO HAS BEEN IMPRISONED SINCE THE OGRE'S CAPTURE OF THE CASTLE.

WAS FÜR EIN ORT IST DAS HIER?

THEN HE, TOO, GOES DOWN BENEATH A STRUGGLING HEAP IN THE DARKNESS.

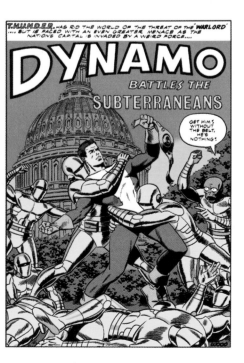

T.HUNDER..HAS RID THE WORLD OF THE THREAT OF THE 'WARLORD' ....BUT IS FACED WITH AN EVEN GREATER MENACE AS THE NATIONS CAPITAL IS INVADED BY A WEIRD FORCE....

DYNAMO
BATTLES THE
SUBTERRANEANS

GET HIM WITHOUT THE BELT, HE'S NOTHING!

who weren't good enough to break into pulp magazines."[19]

In one particular story, for the *Three Aces* aviation strip in a 1941 issue of *Action Comics*, Chad borrowed heavily from a 1940 *Prince Valiant* sequence. In Foster's work, Val had spent several Sundays involved with a literal giant of a man. For his strip, Grothkopf swiped the figures of the giant, turning him into an ancient Mayan. The introductory splash panel of the *Three Aces* story is a pretty straightforward swipe.[20] But for many of the panels that followed, Chad utilized mirror images of Val's giant in rendering his Mayan guardian.[21]

Frank Frazetta needs little introduction to lovers of heroic illustration. His paintings of Conan for Lancer Books launched a wave of sword-&-sorcery fiction in the 1960s. A natural talent who began drawing at the age of two, Frazetta soaked up influences like a sponge—from the early Walt Disney animated features to the energy of Elsie Segar's *Popeye* and Jack Kirby's *Captain America*. "If you know where to look, one can easily see all these influences mysteriously mixed and transformed in the art of Frazetta," wrote Frazetta's friend, Dr. David Winiewicz. "Frank looked at the early *Tarzan* novels before he could even read; he loved the pictures by [J. Allen] St. John. He also marveled at the newspaper strip art of Hal Foster. When he got the *Tarzan Single Series* #20 comic book, he said it was like the *Encyclopedia Britannica*."[22]

Given Frazetta's love of Foster's early work, it's not too surprising to see some of it creep into his art on the Tarzan-like Thun'da. Published by Magazine Enterprises early in 1952, *Thun'da, King of the Congo* features 32 pages of prime early Frazetta, filled with pterodactyls, cavemen, and lost civilizations. At this late date, we have no idea of the deadline pressures Frank faced, but two panels of the issue's second story strongly suggest panels from Foster's *Tarzan of the Apes,* Strip #37.[23]

Everett Raymond Kinstler is one of American's great artists. He has painted the portraits of over a thousand famous individuals, not only of the stage and screen, but also of government and academia. Seven presidents of the United States have sat for Kinstler, and his paintings of Gerald Ford and Ronald Reagan became those Presidents' official White House portraits.

Perhaps less well known is the fact that Kinstler got his start drawing for pulp magazines and comic books. While still in his teens, he drew pen & ink illustrations for *The Shadow*. After World War II, he even drew a couple of *Hawkman* stories. And, yes, he swiped from Foster, too.

In illustrating a science-fiction comic book for Avon Periodicals,[24] Kinstler swiped a scene from an early 1937 *Prince Valiant* page.

Wallace Wood could draw just about anything. Humor, Westerns, romance, horror, adventure, super-heroes, you name it and Woody

The cover for Hartmuth - Der junge Held *#7, 1955, and panels by Milo Manara (*Jolanda de Almaviva*) and Wally Wood (*T.H.U.N.D.E.R. Agents *#3, 1966) are "tributes" to Foster.*

ONE BY ONE HER DREAM CASTLES TUMBLE ABOUT HER EARS. SHE WANTS TO MARRY A PRINCE, NOT A LIGHT-HEARTED BUTCHER. SHE WANTS TO SIT ON THE THRONE OF THULE, NOT ON A WAR-HORSE IN FOGGY ENGLAND. IN FACT, WHAT SHE WANTS MOST OF ALL, SHE DECIDES, IS TO BE LOVED BY · · · ·

SHIERA, THE HAWKMAN'S FRIEND PREPARES TO VISIT HIM . . .

I HAVEN'T HEARD FROM THE HAWK LATELY. THINK I'LL WALK OVER TO HIS HOME.

I DON'T **HAVE** ANY QUESTIONS.

could draw it. His work for EC Comics—in just about all of the aforementioned categories—is still studied and revered, decades later. Wood worked for nearly every comics publishing house that was in business from the 1940s to the '80s, including a memorable stint for Tower Comics, where he wrote, drew, and edited *T.H.U.N.D.E.R. Agents*, assisted by a number of other artists.

Part collaborator/part instructor, Wood had developed a set of rules for his assistants: "Never draw what you can copy. Never copy what you can trace. And never trace what you can cut out and paste up."[25]

"Woody had filing cabinets packed with folders of his swipe files, images he'd cut from newspapers, comic books, and magazines," recalled Steranko. "He had amassed the 'morgue' from his youth through the Thunder Agents period, when he and his assistants really plundered the material. They'd copy Raymond or Fine or Crandall, and Woody would ink, magically transforming anything beneath his pen to a Wood image because he was such a powerful, idiosyncratic stylist."[26]

On at least one occasion, Wood's morgue provided a pose for T.H.U.N.D.E.R.'s lead agent Dynamo[27] that was more than a little evocative of Prince Valiant. In this case, Dan Adkins was the assistant who dug out the appropriate swipe. In 2001, Adkins reminisced about working on the story, "that

Rob Møhlmann
Prins Valiants Zwartboek OVER PLAGIAAT

DRUKWERK

one about robots coming up in Washington, D.C. with that big shot of the Capitol on the splash page. [Wally] would lay it out ... the figures were mostly there, all you had to do was tighten them up, they were most of the time on the money. He said if I could find a better figure, to swipe it."[28]

It's no surprise that Woody's assistants would find *Prince Valiant* reference in his files. Foster had always been a major influence on him. Starting with a parody strip in the mid-1950s,[29] Wood was able to openly ape Foster's Valiant countless times for EC's *Mad* over the years. And in the 1970s, he was even given the opportunity to ghost a *Prince Valiant* page, written by Foster himself.[30] It's hard to imagine a better accolade.

Harold R. "Hal" Foster began his career as a newspaper cartoonist in 1928, with an adaptation of Edgar Rice Burroughs's *Tarzan of the Apes*. Almost a decade later, he would create *Prince Valiant*, a weekly Sunday comics page which continues to this day, having outlived its creator by thirty-four years and counting.

And if you're wondering why he's included in this listing, it's because Foster himself occasionally used swipes.

Don't believe me? Take a close look at Frederic Remington's "The Cowboy."

"The Cowboy" was one of a series of paintings by Remington that saw print in the October 1902 issue of *Scribner's Magazine*.[31] In his time, Remington was a painter and sculptor renowned for his depictions of the American West of the late nineteenth century. There are few artists who could capture a man on horseback so well.

Top: Foster from 1939 compared to Moldoff in Flash *#7, 1940; and Jeffrey Catherine Jones's "Idyll" from* National Lampoon, *Oct., 1975.*

Left: Prince Valiant's Black Book about Plagerism (Prins Valiants zwartboek over plagiaat) by Rob Møhlmann was a 144-page book published in 1982 by Drukwerk that focused almost exclusively on Dutch artists who swiped Foster. Among the artists included were Henk Sprenger, Willy Vandersteen, and Jan Waterschoot who was one of the best Flemish realistic illustrators.

Right: Foster's 1928, Tarzan *comic strip, and Joe Kubert's retelling of the origin of the Lord of the Jungle in* Tarzan of the Apes *#207, 1972.*

Now check out Panel 6 of Foster's *Prince Valiant* for May 24, 1953. The pose, the shadows, even much of the rendering of Valiant's mount are a mirror image of the horse and its rider in "The Cowboy." Just as Chad Grothkopf had reversed images from *Prince Valiant* for his swipes, so had Foster borrowed from Remington.

So, what have we learned from all this? Well, I don't know about you, but after poring over dozens of sources in preparation for this little review, I've come away with an even greater appreciation of Hal Foster's work and the influence he has had on generations of comics artists. As someone whose artistic skills never advanced beyond the ability to draw simple stick figures, I have always been in awe of artists, and Foster was clearly one of the best.

Then, there is the matter of swiping. Certainly, copying another artist's work—physically experiencing how someone else has solved a problem of composition or storytelling—can be a learning exercise. As noted earlier, fine-art students have been doing this for generations. And in the wild frontier of the Golden Age of Comic Books, when many budding artists were literally learning on the job, some of them copied the art of others to make up for deficiencies in their own work. Most of them honed their craft, keeping their influences but leaving the swipes behind. Others, not so much.

Dealing with all the myriad legal and ethical questions of swiping could fill the rest of this book, and I'm sure you'd much rather read

IT IS THE SHIP OF ANGOR WRACK, THE SEA-KING, AND ANGOR WRACK NEEDS MORE SLAVES TO PULL THE SWEEPS.

Nay, to Gwynwyn are we pledged ... and to the brave lords and ladies therein – our fate is one. Take now my message to Harald and spare not thy mount!"

THE BEAUTY OF SOMBELENE IS LIKE A STARRY NIGHT. HER DARK EYES MAKE AGED MEN THINK OF SPLENDID DEEDS THEY ONCE HAD MEANT TO DO, AND ROBBED YOUNG MEN OF PEACE FOR-EVERMORE. POETS SIMPLY TORE UP THEIR INADEQUATE VERSES.

Left: Both Angor Wrack and Sombelene from *Prince Valiant* (1941) made "appearances" in Roy G. Krenkel's tryout page for a proposed Sunday comic strip, *Gwynwyn* (dated 3-27-1947). It seems the final sentence; "Take now my message to Harald…" is a not-so-subtle wink to Harold R. Foster.

IN FAR OFF PANNONIA THE NEWS OF VAL'S RAIDS CAUSES GREAT ANGER. *"THE HUN MUST BE FEARED AND RESPECTED!"* CRIES THE GREAT KHAN AND CALLS UP AN ARMY.

NEXT WEEK: **TROUBLE!**

THE COOL SPARKLING WATER FEELS SO GOOD ON HIS BRUISED AND WEARY BODY THAT HE FAILS TO NOTICE THE CROUCHING FIGURE CREEPING CLOSER.

LOOKING DOWN UPON THEIR ENEMY'S PREPARATIONS, THEY ESTIMATE THAT IT WILL BE TWO MOONS BEFORE THEY ARE READY TO ATTACK. WITH THE ODDS ALREADY 20 TO 1 AGAINST THEM, THE "HUN-HUNTERS" POSITION WILL BE HOPELESS IF THEY ARE ATTACKED FROM THE REAR ALSO.

EARTHEN FORT

I..I SHALL BE THE FIRST RULER OF ALL THE WORLD!

DURING THE TERRIFIC DAYTIME HEAT... THE HAWK RESTS AT A DESERT LAKE

I CAN SPOT THESE LITTLE LAKES FROM UP IN THE SKY. AT THIS RATE I'LL SOON BE THERE.

THE HAWK SOON COMES TO THE GREAT DESERT, ACROSS WHICH LIES ALAMUT, CITY OF THE ASSASSINS...

THE BLISTERING SANDS OFFER NO PROBLEM TO THE MAN THAT CAN FLY *OVER* THEM..

Above: More panels from the "Hawkman" story in Flash *#7, 1940, compared to previously published* Prince Valiant *pages. Note that the upper left inset panel in Foster's version is from a completely different page; however, Moldoff appropriated it to fit his story.*

Below: This particular Prince Valiant *panel from 1941 was first used by Seymour "Sy" Barry in* The Phantom *in 1967, and has been redrawn numerous times over the years whenever the character's origin is retold.*

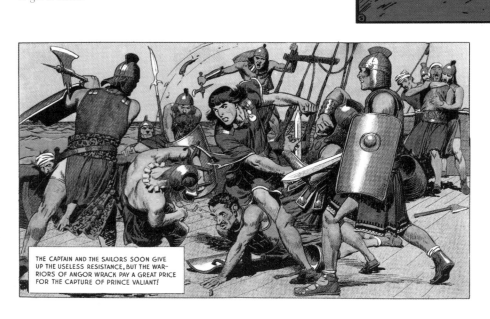

THE CAPTAIN AND THE SAILORS SOON GIVE UP THE USELESS RESISTANCE, BUT THE WAR-RIORS OF ANGOR WRACK PAY A GREAT PRICE FOR THE CAPTURE OF PRINCE VALIANT!

THE NEMESIS OF ALL EVILDOERS – THE PHANTOM FOUGHT ESPECIALLY AGAINST PIRATES – THROUGH THE CENTURIES – ON THE SPANISH MAIN –

the latest volume of *Prince Valiant*. So, let us close with a provocative rule of thumb that has been applied to many disciplines. In the field of illustration, it was summed up well by the great 20th Century portraitist and teacher Joseph Cummings Chase: "On the title page of most of the books on Art should be printed, 'If you steal from one person it's plagiarism: if you steal from three persons it's research.'"[32]

That said, let us now return to the days of King Arthur for Volume 14 of *Prince Valiant*.

Roger Stern
May 13, 2016

Roger Stern has written for comic strips, comic books, radio, television, the stage, and the Internet, creating scripts for everything from sketch comedy to flash-animation. For ten years, he was the senior writer of the Superman series for DC Comics. Stern has written hundreds of stories about such diverse characters as the Atom, Green Lantern, Supergirl, Starman, and the Justice League for DC Comics; and Spider-Man, Doctor Strange, Captain America, Iron Man, the Incredible Hulk, and the Avengers for Marvel. His first novel, *The Death and Life of Superman*, was a New York Times bestseller.

The Author would like to thank Anonymous (Carl Horak?),[33] Terry Beatty, Jeff Hetzel, Brian Kane, and Carmela Merlo for their help and contributions to this Foreword. He would also like to thank Mom and Dad for buying him a copy of Jules Feiffer's *The Great Comic Book Heroes*, all those years ago. Best Christmas present ever.

Additional thanks to Michael T. Gilbert, Axel M. Wulff, Ron Marz, Victor Lim and Bryan Shedden for supplying several of the illustrations accompanying this article.

ENDNOTES

1   Jim Steranko, http://sterankopedia.tumblr.com/ (July 23, 2013)

2   There was also the fact that it ran only on Sundays. And it was the only comic strip in our paper, other than *Ferd'nand*, that didn't use word balloons.

3   Jules Feiffer, *The Great Comic Book Heroes* (New York, The Dial Press, 1965), page 38.

4   Roy Thomas, "A Moon...A Bat...A Hawk: A Candid Conversation with Sheldon Moldoff," *Alter Ego* Volume 3, #4 (Spring, 2000), pages 6-7.

5   Untitled Story, *Detective Comics* #31 (September, 1939), page 1, panel 2.

6   "The Batman Wars Against the Dirigible of Doom," *Detective Comics* #33 (November 1939), page 2, panel 9; subsequently reprinted in *Batman* #1 (Spring, 1940).

7   Untitled Story, *Detective Comics* #34 (December, 1939), page 3, panel 3.

8   Sheldon Moldoff, *The Golden Age Hawkman Archives, Volume One* (New York, DC Comics, 2005), page 5.

9   Feiffer, page 39.

10   Untitled Story, *Flash Comics* #5 (May, 1940), *Hawkman*, pages 5, 7, and 9, as cited by Anonymous (Carl Horak?) in Untitled Article, Source Unknown. See also, footnote 33.

11   Untitled Story, *Flash Comics* #7 (May, 1940), Hawkman, pages 4 and 6, *op.cit.*

12   Untitled Story, *Action Comics* #42 (November, 1941), *Black Pirate*, pages 1-2, *op. cit.*

13   Gary Groth, "Jack Kirby Interview," *The Comics Journal* #134 (February, 1990); as archived at http://www.tcj.com/jack-kirby-portrait-interview/ (May 23, 2011).

14   Jim Steranko, http://sterankopedia.tumblr.com/ (July 24, 2013)

15   *Red Raven Comics* #1 (August, 1940), Cover.

16   Harry Mendryk, "Jack Kirby, Fanboy," http://kirbymuseum.org/blogs/simonandkirby/archives/2198 (August 28, 2009)

17   Mark Evanier, "Introduction," in *Jack Kirby's The Demon* (New York, DC Comics, 2008), page 2.

18   Howard Beckerman, *Animation: The Whole Story* (New York, Allworth Press, 2003)

19   Jim Scancarelli, "I Believed in What I Did," in *The Fawcett Companion* (Raleigh, North Carolina, TwoMorrows Publishing, 2001), page 112.

20   "The Ancient One," *Action Comics* #36 (May, 1941), *Three Aces*, Page 1; as cited by Anonymous (Carl Horak?) in Untitled Article, Source Unknown.

21   "The Ancient One," page 4, *op. cit.*

22   Dr. David Winiewicz, http://fritzfrazetta.blogspot.com/2011/09/frazetta-and-hal-foster.html (September 21, 2011)

23   "The Monsters from the Mists," *Thun'da, King of the Congo* #1 (1952), page 7, panels 4 & 6.

24   *Strange Worlds* #6 (February, 1952), Frontispiece, as cited by Terry Beatty, http://www.scaryterrysworld.com/2010/07/strange-worlds-wally-wood-ray-kinstler.html (July 8, 2010)

25   As quoted countless times by numerous assistants.

26   Jim Steranko, http://sterankopedia.tumblr.com/ July 24, 2013.

27   "Dynamo battles the Subterraneans," *T.H.U.N.D.E.R. Agents* #3 (March, 1966), page 1.

28   Jon B. Cooke, "Dan Adkins Interview: Dynamite Dan's Days of T.H.U.N.D.E.R.," *Comic Book Artist* #14 (July, 2001), Page 35.

29   "Prince Violent," *Mad* #13 (July, 1954).

30   *Prince Valiant* # 1762, as noted by Todd Goldberg, Carl Horak, & Brian M. Kane in *The Definitive Prince Valiant Companion*, (Seattle, WA, Fantagraphics Books, 2009), page 44.

31   Bruce Johnson, http://hoocher.com/Frederic_Remington/Frederic_Remington.htm (undated)

32   Joseph Cummings Chase, "Do You Call THAT Art?" *The Commentator*, (October, 1938), page 26 ... though, it should be noted, we originally found Chase's words at http://quoteinvestigator.com/2010/09/20/plagiarism/#more-1178. (Thanks, Q.I.!)

33   In February of 2016, Brian Kane sent me a copy of a short article he had acquired, which pointed out a number of early swipes from *Prince Valiant*. It was of great help in tracking down those swipes, several of which we have noted in this Foreword. Unfortunately, the article was both untitled and unsigned. Brian is still at a loss as to where it was published—or *if* it was ever published—and has forgotten who even sent it to him. Foster Indexer Todd Goldberg thinks it might have been written by the late Carl Horak, but we have been unable to verify that. To whomever the Anonymous Author may be, you have our deepest thanks.

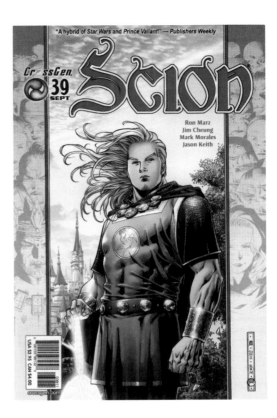

Top: "Prince Valiant *was certainly in the DNA of* Scion. *The initial broad strokes of the concept were put together by CrossGen's founder and owner, Mark Alessi, and* Prince Valiant *was mentioned as a touchstone. Obviously I took that and ran with it, not so much for specifics, but more for the overall tone. One review compared* Scion *to a mixture of* Prince Valiant *and* Star Wars, *which I suppose is pretty accurate. There was a set of* Prince Valiant *reprint volumes in Alessi's office, and* Scion's *artist, Jim Cheung, drew a lot of inspiration from them. Certainly issue #39 was the culmination of that. We wanted to pay homage to Foster and the glory of his Sunday pages."*

—Ron Marz

Bottom: *Even Hal Foster swiped on occasion. Featuring Frederick Remington's* The Cowboy *(1902) compared to a* Prince Valiant *panel from 1953.*

IN SUDDEN DESPERATION THE ARMY TURNS AND MARCHES ON PLYMOUTH IN THE HOPE OF OBTAINING FOOD THERE. VAL SEES THE MANEUVER AND RACES AHEAD.

MIGHT FOR RIGHT: A CODE OF HONOR FOR SENTINELS OF LIBERTY

Addendum by Brian M. Kane

Several years ago, shortly after Fantagraphics began this series of *Prince Valiant* reprints, someone commented online that they could not discern Foster's visual legacy—his impact on the comics medium. Certainly there was the Noel Sickles/Milton Caniff/Alex Toth family, and the Alex Raymond/Al Williamson /Thomas Yeates lineage, but Foster? Somehow Wally Wood, Frank Frazetta and the rest of the Fleagles vanished from memory.

Clearly Raymond and Caniff were the progenitors of illustrative style-schools, but what about Foster? Who aped Foster's style? Well, no one. No one in comics had that level of artistic skill, so no one tried. Yet that did not stop people from swiping Foster because what they appropriated from *Tarzan* and *Prince Valiant* were a master artisan's forms and compositions—not his "style". When Bob Kane, Jack Kirby, Frank Frazetta, and Don Rosa swiped Foster they were making no allusions to being part of Foster's legacy; they were simply adapting his panel designs to their own needs; their own style. Foster's visual legacy is not readily apparent because it is hiding in plain sight. For Kirby it hid in the iconography of his Asgardian and Fourth World costumes, and in those massive battle scenes he did so well.

Yet there is more to Prince Valiant than artistic style. At his core Val is a born leader with an unerring sense of fairness; exuding curiosity, nobility, humor, confidence, optimism, and intelligence all wrapped in a cocky swagger that makes him *real*. There is a "Might for Right!" mentality at work with Val that is decidedly not Arthurian; at least not one found in the classic writings of Geoffrey of Monmouth or Sir Thomas Malory. That aphorism was coined by T.H. White in *The Once and Future King*, so it did not exist until 1958

(and in its adaptation, *Camelot* on Broadway in 1960). You could say, the concept of "Might for Right!", as it is expressed in *Prince Valiant*, is a Fosterism. Val has a code of honor, which speaks to helping the weak and oppressed, to seeing the good in people—especially those who are different from us, to bringing the wrong-doers to justice, and to standing up for what is right even when the odds are against you. In 1937, before the first superhero comic book hit the stands, Val presented a moral template for heroes who fought against ignorance and oppression as beacons of hope—heroes like Captain America.

Understand that Jack Kirby was just 19 years old when *Prince Valiant* premiered in the color Saturday comics (Val did not graduate to the Sunday color supplement until page #66, 5-15-38). At that time the publication of *Captain America* #1 was still four years away. We know that Kirby had a deep respect for Foster that lasted decades; *The Demon* is emblematic of that, so Val's colorful adventures had an immediate effect on the young artist, and the development of Captain America. Clearly Val and Cap are both soldiers, both are brilliant military strategists, both dress in red, white and blue, wear chainmail shirts, and have a round shield with a symbol on it denoting their nationality (which also appears on their chests), but it is Captain America's code of honor that makes him a philosophical offspring of Prince Valiant. Cap's sense of morality, idealism, and tenacity for seeking truth, justice, and those other things are what make him and Val heroic. Both Cap and Val jump headlong into a conflict confident that righteousness will prevail and they will win the day.

While Val substantially inspired the development of Cap's morality, Foster's tales also influenced Joe Simon's and Jack Kirby's

storytelling. Several of Cap's earliest stories noticeably show their sources. In "The Hunchback of Hollywood and the Movie Murder" (*Captain America* #3), Cap becomes a film knight then later gets into a sword fight with a villain sporting a Prince Valiant hairdo; in "Ivan the Terrible" (*Captain America* #4), Bucky dreams that he and Cap save the exiled King Peter Ross and restore him to his throne (see panel below); and in "Case of the Black Witch" (*Captain America* #8), Cap and Bucky face hordes of nightmarish creatures not unlike those created by Morgan Le Fey to attack Val (*Prince Valiant*, page 58, 3-19-38). They are all fun tributes from the man who would be "King" to his "Prince".

Yet there is one thing that definitely sets Val and Cap apart. Only one of them has a magical weapon. Prince Valiant's charmed *Singing Sword, Flamberge* was "made by the same mage who forged King Arthur's sword *Excalibur*" (*Prince Valiant*, page 92, 11-13-38). Yet, while we have seen the witch, Horrit, shriek in terror from it, that is the extent of its powers under Foster's guidance. However, Captain America's shield is imbued with magic that cannot be described because it always defies the laws of physics; bouncing around as if possessed by a demon only to unerringly return to its master—not unlike Thor's hammer, *Mjölnir*. While I am sure Foster was satisfied with the mythology he wove for his hero...just think of what Prince Valiant could have done if he had Captain America's shield!

SOMETIME LATER, THE THREE FUGITIVES REACH THE CAVE WHERE THE EXILED KING AND HIS FOLLOWERS ARE HIDING--

CAPTAIN AMERICA AND BUCKY, THIS IS MY FATHER, KING PETER ROSS.

Prince Valiant
IN THE DAYS OF KING ARTHUR
WRITTEN AND ILLUSTRATED BY HAROLD R. FOSTER

Our Story: A FAIR WIND BLOWS AND THE VOYAGE TO CAMELOT BEGINS. THE SHIP IS CROWDED WITH THE GUARD FOR THE TREASURE CHESTS, THE HORSES, PRINCE VALIANT, HIS FAMILY AND THE GUESTS.

ETHWALD PROVES TO BE A VERY ENTERTAINING GUEST AND REGALES THEM WITH TALES OF HUNTING ADVENTURES IN THE WEALD, THAT GREAT FOREST REGION NEAR HIS FIEF.

THE SHIP IS WALLOWING UP THE CHANNEL WHEN THE WATER CASKS SPRING A MYSTERIOUS LEAK. "I KNOW A SHELTERED COVE WHERE THE CASKS CAN BE FILLED FROM A SPARKLING BROOK," OFFERS ETHWALD.

IT IS JUST AS HE SAID, AND THE CASKS ARE TOWED ASHORE TO BE FILLED. ETHWALD AND HIS FRIENDS PROPOSE A FEW HOURS OF HUNTING TO PASS THE TIME AWAY, AND INVITE ARN TO JOIN THEM.

THE PARTY REACHES THE TOP OF THE DOWNS AND SEES THE GREAT FOREST OF THE WEALD STRETCHING INTO THE DISTANCE. "LOOK, THERE IS A STRONGHOLD ON YONDER HILL," SAYS ARN, POINTING.
"WHOSE IS IT?"
"MINE," ANSWERS ETHWALD SLYLY, AND, AT HIS SIGNAL, ARN IS SEIZED.

THE CASKS HAVE BEEN FILLED AND STOWED LONG SINCE. THE DAY IS ENDING, AND YET NO SIGN OF THE HUNTING PARTY. VAL AND ALETA ARE WORRIED.

1452.

A SKIFF PUTS OUT FROM SHORE; A NOTE IS DELIVERED AND THE BOATMAN PULLS AWAY IN THE DARKNESS. A RANSOM NOTE!

1-6-63

AND ARN, LOCKED IN A DUSTY ROOM, WONDERS IF HE WILL EVER BE ABLE TO TRUST ANYONE ANY MORE.

NEXT WEEK- Cough Medicine

Our Story: PRINCE VALIANT READS THE LETTER DEMANDING RANSOM FOR HIS SON ARN. THEN HE GATHERS ALL AVAILABLE FIGHTING MEN AND, IN A TOWERING RAGE, GOES TO FIND SIEUR ETHWALD'S STRONGHOLD.

ETHWALD GREETS THEM CHEERFULLY. "GOOD DAY, SIR VALIANT. AS YOU VERY WELL KNOW YOU HAVE NOT SUFFICIENT MEN TO STORM THESE WALLS, BUT IF YOU WILL LEAVE YOUR ARMS OUTSIDE, YOU MAY ENTER IN SAFETY TO DISCUSS A MATTER OF BUSINESS."

"YOUR SON, PRINCE ARN, IS A FINE LAD. YOU MUST BE VERY PROUD OF HIM. HE IS WELL WORTH THE TREASURE CHESTS YOU HAVE ABOARD YOUR SHIP." AND ETHWALD LAUGHS PLEASANTLY AND ORDERS REFRESHMENTS.

VAL RETURNS TO THE SHIP. "PAY THE RANSOM AND GET ARN BACK," ADVISES ALETA, "THEN LAY SIEGE BEFORE THE WALLS UNTIL WE CAN SUMMON HELP FROM THE KING." VAL SHAKES HIS HEAD, "THE TREASURE IS IN MY SAFEKEEPING AND IS NOT MINE TO GIVE."

"WELL, THE LEAST YOU CAN DO IS SEND ARN THE MEDICINE FOR HIS COLD," ALETA SNAPS, "EVEN IF HE DOES COMPLAIN IT TASTES LIKE POISON."

1353

AS HE WATCHES ALETA BUSY WITH HER MEDICINE CHEST AN IDEA IS FORMING IN HIS MIND.

1-13-63

AND SOON THEY ARE CONCOCTING A BITTER BUT ALMOST HARMLESS POTION THEY HOPE WILL CURE ETHWALD OF HIS GREED.
NEXT WEEK- Sleight-of-Hand

Prince Valiant
IN THE DAYS OF KING ARTHUR
WRITTEN AND ILLUSTRATED BY HAROLD R FOSTER

Our Story: PRINCE VALIANT CLIMBS THE CLIFF TO ETHWALD'S STRONGHOLD TO ARRANGE RANSOM FOR THE RETURN OF HIS SON, ARN, AND HE CARRIES A VIAL OF NAUSEATING CHEMICALS UNDER HIS GREAT CAPE.

WHEN HE STATES HIS MISSION HE IS ADMITTED AND STANDS BEFORE THE TRIUMPHANT ETHWALD.

"THE CLIMB UP THE CLIFF HAS MADE ME THIRSTY," SAYS VAL. HIS HOST ORDERS WINE TO BE SERVED. HE IS IN A JOVIAL MOOD, FOR WILL HE NOT SOON BE RICH?

UNDER COVER OF HIS CLOAK VAL EMPTIES THE VIAL INTO HIS HALF-EMPTY GOBLET.

"ON YONDER KNOLL RANSOM AND HOSTAGE WILL BE EXCHANGED," AND VAL DRAWS ETHWALD'S ATTENTION AWAY LONG ENOUGH FOR HIM TO SWITCH THE GOBLETS.

"MUCH AS I ABHOR CRIME I MUST DRINK TO YOUR CLEVERNESS." THEN VAL DRAINS HIS GLASS.

1354

ETHWALD DOES LIKEWISE. A PUZZLED LOOK CROSSES HIS FACE, HIS MOUTH TWISTS IN A GRIMACE; HE GAZES WITH STARING EYES AT THE CRYSTALS ON THE BOTTOM OF HIS GOBLET. "POISON!" HE CRIES.

1-20-63

"YES," ANSWERS VAL PLEASANTLY, "YOU HAVE TWO VERY UNPLEASANT DAYS TO LIVE, BUT QUEEN ALETA, WHO IS SKILLED IN CHEMISTRY, MIGHT GIVE YOU AN ANTIDOTE. AT A PRICE, OF COURSE."

NEXT WEEK - The Cure

HAL FOSTER

Prince Valiant
IN THE DAYS OF KING ARTHUR
WRITTEN AND ILLUSTRATED BY HAROLD R FOSTER

Our Story: "I HAVE BEEN POISONED!" CROAKS ETHWALD HOARSELY. "GUARDS, SEIZE PRINCE VALIANT." THEN TURNING TO VAL HE WHEEZES, "YOU AND YOUR SON WILL DIE UNLESS THE ANTIDOTE AND THE TREASURE ARE SENT TO ME AT ONCE."
"YOU KNOW HOW THESE CLEVER WOMEN ARE," ANSWERS VAL CHEERFULLY. "THEY ARE NOT TO BE TRUSTED."

"THE QUEEN HAS A TERRIBLE TEMPER," LIES VAL. "DO NOT ANGER HER, SHE MIGHT SAIL AWAY WITH BOTH THE ANTIDOTE AND THE TREASURE. SHALL WE GO TO HER AT ONCE?"

"VERY WELL, BUT I WILL HOLD YOUR SON, ARN, AS HOSTAGE FOR MY SAFE RETURN."
VAL IS QUITE SYMPATHETIC. "OH, ETHWALD, DO NOT TEMPT FATE. ALREADY THE POISON IS EATING AWAY YOUR ENTRAILS AND IT IS NO TIME TO QUIBBLE."

"IF YOU DO NOT RETURN HER SON, THE QUEEN WILL BE WROTH AND WILL MOST LIKELY GIVE YOU A MORE POWERFUL POISON INSTEAD OF THE ANTIDOTE." AND ETHWALD, NOW IN THE GRIP OF FEAR, HAS ARN RELEASED.

HE PLEADS WITH ALETA FOR AN IMMEDIATE CURE, BUT, BEING A WOMAN, SHE HAS QUITE A LOT TO SAY ABOUT DELINQUENT KNIGHTS, AND NOTHING CAN STOP HER.

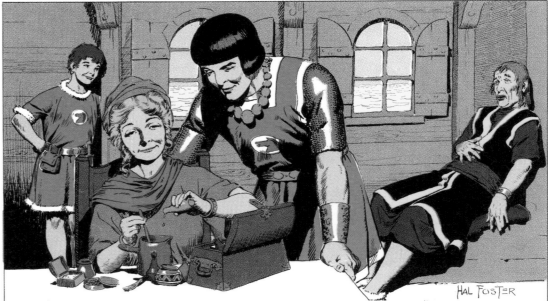

"WHAT WAS THE 'POISON' YOU GAVE HIM?" ASKS VAL. ALETA GIGGLES: "MUSTARD, ALUM AND BITTER ROOT."
"NO WONDER HE THOUGHT HIMSELF POISONED," SAYS VAL. "AND WHAT WILL YOUR SO-CALLED ANTIDOTE CONSIST OF?"
"RANCID FISH OIL, WORMWOOD, HONEY AND GALL," ANSWERS ALETA SWEETLY, "TO BE TAKEN EVERY HOUR."

HAL FOSTER

1355.

NEXT WEEK - **The Hero**

1-27-63

Prince Valiant
IN THE DAYS OF KING ARTHUR
WRITTEN AND ILLUSTRATED BY HAROLD R FOSTER

Our Story: ETHWALD IS CONVINCED THAT HE HAS BEEN POISONED, AND WITH GOOD REASON; FOR THE POTION ALETA HAD CONCOCTED FOR HIM WILL GUARANTEE HIM CRAMPS FOR SOME TIME.

BUT SHE HAS GRACIOUSLY CONSENTED TO MIX AN ANTIDOTE, WHICH IS WORSE. RANCID FISH OIL, SALT, GALL, MUSTARD AND HONEY ARE AMONG THE INGREDIENTS. AFTER A GENEROUS DOSE OF THIS 'CURE' HE LEAVES THE CABIN...

....WHILE LEANING OVER THE RAIL ETHWALD DISCOVERS THAT THE SHIP'S BOATS ARE TOWING THE VESSEL OUT OF THE COVE TO THE OPEN SEA.

HE ACCUSES ALETA OF TREACHERY! NOW, THIS IS THE WRONG THING TO SAY TO A MOTHER WHOSE SON HE HAS HELD FOR RANSOM. PRINCE VALIANT, A MARRIED MAN OF SOME EXPERIENCE, MAKES AN EFFORT TO SAVE HIM, BUT TOO LATE!

AN HOUR PASSES DURING WHICH POOR ETHWALD LEARNS ALL ABOUT THE FLAWS IN HIS CHARACTER AND MANY MORE HE DID NOT EVEN SUSPECT. HE ALSO LEARNS THAT HE IS BEING TAKEN TO CAMELOT AND THE KING'S JUSTICE.

ONCE AGAIN PRINCE VALIANT RETURNS TO CAMELOT A HERO, A QUEST WELL DONE. THE AWFUL PILGRIMAGE IS OVER, THE TREASURE FOR THE ABBEY DELIVERED SAFELY

1356.

HAL FOSTER

NOW ALETA HAS WORK TO DO. THIS SMUG AND POMPOUS HERO MUST BE REDUCED TO THE MODEST, ATTENTIVE HUSBAND SHE LOVES SO WELL.

NEXT WEEK- **War Clouds**

2-3-63

Our Story: FOR TWO MONTHS NOW WAR CLOUDS HAVE SHADOWED THE NORTH COUNTRY, YET KING ARTHUR SEEMINGLY DOES NOTHING. BUT NOW THE TIME HAS COME ONCE AGAIN TO SECURE THE REALM, AND HIS IMPATIENT KNIGHTS ARE EAGER FOR THE FRAY.

PROMOTION COMES TO A YOUNG PAGE. ARN IS SUMMONED BEFORE SIR BALDWIN AND INFORMED THAT HE IS NOW A NOVICE AND MAY TRAIN FOR COMBAT.

YOUNG NOBLES MUST SERVE AS PAGE BOYS TO LEARN COURTLY MANNERS, BUT ARN HAS BEEN TAUGHT COURTESY SINCE CHILDHOOD. IT IS DOUBTFUL IF ANY OTHER PAGE HAS RECEIVED BETTER INSTRUCTION IN OBEDIENCE, RESPECT AND CHIVALRY THAN HE .....

..... NOR DOES ANY NOVICE HAVE A BETTER OR MORE SEVERE TEACHER. OVER AND OVER HE SPEEDS DOWN THE COURSE WITH LANCE OR SWORD UNTIL HORSE AND RIDER BECOME AS ONE.

THEN SIR BALDWIN SEES HIM PERFORM AND AGAIN PROMOTES HIM, THIS TIME TO BACHELOR. ARN IS THE YOUNGEST OF THIS GROUP AND TAKES MANY A BEATING.

THE WEARY, PAINFUL DAYS DRAG BY, THE LUMPS AND BRUISES MULTIPLY, BUT AT LAST HE GETS THE REWARD HE HAS BEEN HOPING FOR: "YOU ARE DOING FAIRLY WELL. WE MAY MAKE A WARRIOR OF YOU YET," HIS SIRE ADMITS.

THE WAR COUNCIL HAS COMPLETED THEIR PLANS, AND THE CAPTAINS ARE CALLED IN TO BE ASSIGNED THEIR DUTIES. AND THEY NOTE WITH SATISFACTION THE SUBTLE CHANGE IN THEIR KING. THIS IS ARTHUR, LEADER OF MEN, THE MOST FEARED WARRIOR IN ALL BRITAIN!

NEXT WEEK- **The Foe**

1357

2-10-63

Prince Valiant

IN THE DAYS OF KING ARTHUR

WRITTEN AND ILLUSTRATED BY HAROLD R FOSTER

Our Story : THE KING OF NORTH WALES DIES, AND HIS SON CIDWIC MOUNTS THE THRONE. AT ONCE HE SUMMONS HIS VASSAL NOBLES, EACH TO BRING A LEVY OF SOLDIERS ON A WAR FOOTING. ONCE NORTH WALES EXTENDED NORTHWARD INTO SCOTLAND, AND IT HAS LONG BEEN HIS AMBITION TO REGAIN THE LOST TERRITORY AND, PERHAPS, ADD MORE.

WITH SOUNDING TRUMPETS AND WAVING BANNERS CIDWIC BEGINS HIS MARCH. ONLY ONE MAJOR OBSTACLE STANDS IN HIS WAY; THE WALLED CITY OF CARLISLE, BUILT LONG AGO BY THE ROMANS TO GUARD THE WESTERN END OF HADRIAN'S WALL

IF CIDWIC TAKES CARLISLE, HE CAN, WITH THE PROMISE OF PLUNDER, ENLIST THE WARBANDS OF THE WILD PICTS AND CALEDONIANS AND CONQUER ALL NORTH BRITAIN.
KING ARTHUR ORDERS A FLEET OF SHIPS WITH SUPPLIES AND VETERAN ARCHERS TO THE BELEAGUERED CITY.

BUT THE ONLY ARMY HE SENDS AGAINST CIDWIC IS A TROOP OF LIGHT CAVALRY, ENGINEERS, MASONS AND BUILDERS UNDER THE COMMAND OF SIR KAY

TO HIS WARRIORS, EAGER FOR ACTION, HE SAYS: "THE SOLDIERS CIDWIC HAS CALLED UP ARE BOUND TO SERVE ONLY FOR THREE MONTHS, THEN THEY MAY RETURN TO THEIR HOMES TO GATHER THEIR HARVEST. WE WILL RIDE WHEN THE HARVEST MOON IS AT THE FULL."

NEXT WEEK- **Sir Kay's Task**

2-17-63

Prince Valiant
IN THE DAYS OF KING ARTHUR
WRITTEN AND ILLUSTRATED BY HAROLD R FOSTER

Our Story: THE ONLY FORCE KING ARTHUR SENDS AGAINST THE AMBITIOUS CIDWIC IS A TROOP OF CAVALRY AND A SMALL ARMY OF WORKMEN UNDER THE COMMAND OF HIS FOSTER-BROTHER, SIR KAY.

ACROSS THE ROAD LEADING TO CIDWIC'S STRONG-HOLD SIR KAY BUILDS A DITCH AND EARTHWORK, WHICH HE HAS TOPPED WITH A WALL. THERE IS NO INTERFERENCE, FOR THERE ARE BUT FEW WARRIORS LEFT IN THE STRONGHOLD.

AND NOW THE CAVALRY RIDES FORTH, STRIKING AT SUPPLY LINES, COMMUNICATIONS AND FORAGING PARTIES.

CIDWIC HEARS OF THESE RAIDS AND IS PLEASED. IF THAT IS ALL KING ARTHUR CAN SEND AGAINST HIM, HE HAS NOTHING TO FEAR. EVEN IF HE LOSES HIS STRONGHOLD, THE CAPTURE OF CARLISLE AND ITS RICHES WILL GIVE HIM ALL THE STRENGTH HE NEEDS.

BUT CARLISLE DOES NOT FALL. SUPPLIED BY SEA WITH FOOD AND TROOPS, IT RESISTS HIS SIEGE.

1359

HAL FOSTER

THE KING SUMMONS PRINCE VALIANT. "ONLY THE HOPE OF PLUNDER HOLDS CIDWIC'S ARMY BEFORE CARLISLE, BUT AUTUMN IS NEAR AND THEY GROW IMPATIENT TO RETURN TO THEIR HOMES. SELECT A TROOP OF FAST YOUNG RIDERS FROM AMONG THE SQUIRES AND BACHELORS TO ACT AS MESSENGERS, AND KEEP ME INFORMED. TELL SIR KAY OUR ARMY WILL MARCH WITHIN THE WEEK."

NEXT WEEK - **The Chosen**

2-24-63

Prince Valiant
IN THE DAYS OF KING ARTHUR
WRITTEN AND ILLUSTRATED BY HAROLD R FOSTER

Our Story: IN THE PRACTICE YARD PRINCE VALIANT WATCHES THE YOUNG SQUIRES AND BACHELORS AT THEIR TRAINING. FROM THESE HE PICKS THE BEST RIDERS FOR HIS MESSENGERS. FOR HE IS TO PRECEDE THE ARMY AND SEND BACK INFORMATION TO THE KING.

AND VAL MUST CHOOSE HIS OWN SON FOR THIS DANGEROUS WORK. THOUGH THE YOUNGEST AND SMALLEST, ARN IS YET THE MOST NIMBLE RIDER OF THE LOT.

BEFORE THE STOUT WALLS OF CARLISLE, CIDWIC KNOWS DEFEAT AS HIS ARMY MELTS AWAY. HIS MEN HAVE SERVED THEIR ALLOTTED TIME AND ARE ANXIOUS TO RETURN TO THEIR FARMS AND VILLAGES TO PREPARE FOR THE COMING WINTER.

BUT CIDWIC IS A MAN OF ACTION. HE ORDERS A SWIFT RETREAT. IF HE CAN REACH HIS STRONGHOLD BEFORE KING ARTHUR'S ARMY ARRIVES, HE MAY HOLD OUT UNTIL WINTER PUTS AN END TO THE FIGHTING. AND HIS ARMY GROWS AS IT CATCHES UP WITH HOME-BOUND STRAGGLERS.

A SCOUT RIDES IN WITH WORD OF THIS MANEUVER. VAL KNOWS THAT IF IT IS SUCCESSFUL THE WAR MAY GO ON FOR ANOTHER YEAR. HE SENDS HIS SWIFTEST MESSENGER TO THE KING.

1360

AND THAT MESSENGER IS ARN.

ONLY SIR KAY'S OUTPOST STANDS BETWEEN CIDWIC AND HIS STRONGHOLD, AND THAT SMALL OUTPOST MUST HOLD OUT UNTIL THE KING ARRIVES.

NEXT WEEK—**Conflict**

3-3-63

Prince Valiant IN THE DAYS OF KING ARTHUR

WRITTEN AND ILLUSTRATED BY HAROLD R. FOSTER

Our Story: FATHER AND SON RIDE IN OPPOSITE DIRECTIONS; ARN TO WARN KING ARTHUR OF CIDWIC'S UNEXPECTED RETREAT FROM CARLISLE.....

....AND PRINCE VALIANT RIDES FURIOUSLY TO HELP SIR KAY DEFEND THE EARTHWORK THAT LIES BETWEEN CIDWIC'S ONRUSHING ARMY AND HIS MOUNTAIN STRONGHOLD.

PRINCE ARN, HIS MESSAGE DELIVERED, DOES NOT LINGER IN THE SAFETY OF THE ADVANCING ARMY, BUT TURNS HIS HORSE AND RACES BACK FOR FURTHER DUTY.

VAL ARRIVES IN TIME. CIDWIC'S STRONGHOLD STANDS BROODING UPON ITS HILLTOP, AND ACROSS THE ROAD SIR KAY'S PALISADE GUARDS THE APPROACHES. IN THE FAR DISTANCE A CLOUD OF DUST GIVES EVIDENCE OF AN APPROACHING ARMY.

SIR KAY IS WARNED IN TIME, THE PALISADES ARE MANNED, AND THE GATE IS CLOSED AS CIDWIC'S ARMY ENCIRCLES THEM LIKE A LIVING TIDE.

BUT NOT BEFORE ONE LONE RIDER ON A SPENT HORSE LIMPS UP TO THE GATE... ...ARN REPORTS FOR DUTY!

1361

HOPING TO CATCH THE DEFENDERS UNPREPARED, CIDWIC ORDERS AN IMMEDIATE ATTACK IN FORCE. FOR WELL HE KNOWS THAT KING ARTHUR'S KNIGHTS ARE WITHIN THREE DAYS' MARCH.

THE FIRST ATTACK FAILS. A HALT IS CALLED, WHILE SCALING LADDERS AND RAMS ARE MADE AND FIRE-ARROWS PREPARED.
NEXT WEEK- **The Lone Archer**

3-10-63

Prince Valiant
IN THE DAYS OF KING ARTHUR
WRITTEN AND ILLUSTRATED BY HAROLD R FOSTER

Our Story: BALKED IN HIS GREAT DREAM OF CONQUEST, CIDWIC IS PREPARED TO TAKE VENGEANCE ON THIS SMALL FORT, AND HE HIMSELF MUST DO HEROIC DEEDS TO REGAIN THE CONFIDENCE OF HIS WARRIORS.

FIRST COMES A RAIN OF FIRE-ARROWS AGAINST THE WOODEN PALISADE AND BUILDINGS. THE FLAMES ARE KEPT UNDER CONTROL UNTIL THE WELL GOES DRY.

RAMS BATTER AT THE GATES AND SOON THE THUNDER OF THEIR BLOWS IS ACCOMPANIED BY THE SPLINTERING OF WOOD.

HEEDLESS OF THEIR LOSSES THEY CROSS THE DITCH WITH SCALING LADDERS AND STORM THE WALLS IN GREAT NUMBERS.

THE HORSES, DRIVEN MAD BY THE FLAMING ARROWS, ARE RELEASED AS THE GATES COME DOWN, AND CRASH THEIR WAY TO FREEDOM OVER THE CRUSHED AND BROKEN BODIES OF THE ENEMY.

THE EXULTANT VOICE OF THE 'SINGING SWORD' CAN BE HEARD AS PRINCE VALIANT DEFENDS THE STAIRWAY, AND WARRIORS FALL LIKE AUTUMN LEAVES BEFORE HIM.

AND FOR GOOD REASON--AN ARCHER IN THE FLAMING TOWER IS MAKING SURE THE ODDS AGAINST HIS SIRE ARE NOT TOO GREAT.

1362.

SO HEAVY ARE THE LOSSES THAT THE ATTACK FALTERS. CIDWIC DRAWS HIS GREAT SWORD. NOW IS THE TIME TO LEAD HIS WARRIORS TO VICTORY!

NEXT WEEK- The Duel

HAL FOSTER

3-17-63

Our Story: THE MOMENT OF VICTORY IS AT HAND. CIDWIC DRAWS HIS SWORD AND ENTERS THE SHATTERED GATE. THEN HE STOPS, APPALLED!

THE COURTYARD HAS BEEN TAKEN, THE TOWER IS AFLAME AND VACANT EXCEPT FOR ONE LONE ARCHER WHO IS SENDING A STREAM OF ARROWS INTO THE THICK OF THE FIGHT.

TWO STAIRWAYS LEAD TO THE GALLERY ABOVE. ON ONE SIDE SIR KAY IS CHARGING A HIGH PRICE FOR ADMISSION......

....AND THE OTHER IS BEING HELD BY PRINCE VALIANT, WHOSE CUSTOMERS HESITATE BEFORE THE GLITTERING 'SINGING SWORD.'

TOWARD THIS STAIRWAY STRIDES CIDWIC, HIS HEART FILLED WITH RAGE AND DESPAIR. HE WILL TAKE THIS OUTPOST, BUT AT SUCH A COST THAT HIS ARMY WILL NEVER BE ABLE TO FACE KING ARTHUR'S WHEN IT ARRIVES.

"SIR VALIANT," HE CALLS, "DARE YOU PIT YOUR SKILL AGAINST MINE?"

IN THE LURID GLARE OF THE FLAMING TOWER THE TWO LEADERS FACE EACH OTHER. THE SHOUTING AND CLASH OF ARMS DIE DOWN. *"I HAVE EVER WISHED TO TEST MY SKILL AGAINST A CELEBRATED CHAMPION,"* SAYS CIDWIC.
"I WILL DO MY BEST TO MAKE THE TEST INTERESTING," ANSWERS VAL.

NEXT WEEK - **The Test**

3-24-63

Prince Valiant
IN THE DAYS OF KING ARTHUR

WRITTEN AND ILLUSTRATED
BY HAROLD R FOSTER

Our Story: AND SO THE EPIC DUEL BEGINS: PRINCE VALIANT, WEARY, BLEEDING AND GASPING FOR BREATH AFTER HOURS OF COMBAT, FACES KING CIDWIC. AND THE YOUNG KING, FRESH AND CONFIDENT, EXHIBITS HIS SKILL.

VAL, CONSERVING HIS STRENGTH, FIGHTS ON THE DEFENSIVE, WHILE CIDWIC, MASTER OF MANY TRICKS, LEAPS TO THE ATTACK; THEN LEAPS BACK, TRYING TO DRAW VAL INTO SOME MISTAKE. VAL STUDIES HIS NIMBLE FOE, SEEKING TO FIND SOME WEAKNESS. OTHER EYES ARE BUSY, TOO.

"HIS RIGHT LEG, SIRE, WATCH HIS RIGHT LEG!" IT IS ARN'S VOICE SPEAKING IN GREEK, HIS MOTHER'S TONGUE, THAT NONE MAY UNDERSTAND HIS WORDS.

TIME AND AGAIN CIDWIC HAS LEAPED BACK TURNING TO THE LEFT, EXPOSING HIS RIGHT LEG BUT PREPARED FOR A COUNTER-STROKE THAT WOULD SEVER VAL'S ARM DID HE STRIKE AT IT. NOW VAL DOES STRIKE. WHEN NEXT CIDWIC MAKES HIS MOVE VAL LEAPS IN, AND HIS SLASHING STROKE FALLS BEFORE CIDWIC CAN RAISE HIS WEAPON FOR THE COUNTER. HE FEELS THE BURNING SHOCK, TRIES TO REGAIN HIS BALANCE, BUT HIS LEG BUCKLES BENEATH HIM AND HE TOPPLES FROM THE GALLERY TO THE COURTYARD BELOW.

NEXT WEEK - **The Spoilsport**

1364.

3-31-63

Prince Valiant
IN THE DAYS OF KING ARTHUR

WRITTEN AND ILLUSTRATED BY HAROLD R FOSTER

Our Story : PRINCE VALIANT WATCHES HIS ADVERSARY CRASH TO THE COURTYARD BELOW WITHOUT ANY FEELING OF JOY AT HIS VICTORY. HE IS NUMB WITH FATIGUE.

CIDWIC IS MILDLY SURPRISED AS HE LIES THERE GAZING AT THE BRIGHT SKY. HE FEELS NO PAIN, ONLY A GREAT WEARINESS. THEN HE CLOSES HIS EYES AND PEACE COMES AT LAST TO THE TURBULENT SPIRIT OF CIDWIC, YOUNG KING OF NORTH WALES.

THE MOMENTARY STILLNESS IS SHATTERED BY A YOUNG VOICE SHOUTING THE BATTLE CRY, "ONWARD! VICTORY! ARTHUR! ARTHUR! ARTHUR!"

THE ENEMY HAD VICTORY WITHIN THEIR GRASP, BUT NOW, WITH THEIR LEADER GONE, THEY HAVE NOTHING TO FIGHT FOR AND ARE DRIVEN FROM THE OUTPOST.

A CLOUD OF DUST AND THE THUNDER OF HOOFS HERALDS THE ARRIVAL OF KING ARTHUR AND HIS KNIGHTS. THEY HAVE RIDDEN ALL NIGHT TO SURPRISE CIDWIC'S ARMY, BUT THAT ARMY IS SCATTERING IN ALL DIRECTIONS, INTENT ONLY ON REACHING THEIR HOMES.

A VERY YOUNG ARCHER MAY BE FORGIVEN A MOMENT OF PRIDE: "THE GREATEST OF WARRIORS, NONE MAY EQUAL HIM IN SKILL OR HARDIHOOD, AND HE IS MY SIRE! AND I, PRINCE ARN, HAVE FOUGHT BY HIS SIDE!"

"WHY DO I ALWAYS HAVE THE MISFORTUNE TO PICK YOU FOR THESE MISSIONS?" GRUMBLES KING ARTHUR, THOUGH THERE IS A TWINKLE IN HIS EYE. "OUR KNIGHTS HAVE TRAINED HARD AND LONG FOR THIS BATTLE; WE HAVE RIDDEN ALL NIGHT ONLY TO FIND YOU HAVE HAD ALL THE FUN. I AM SORRY TO SAY THIS, SIR VALIANT, BUT YOU ARE A SPOILSPORT!"

NEXT WEEK— **Long live the King**

1365.   4-7-63

Prince Valiant
IN THE DAYS OF KING ARTHUR
WRITTEN AND ILLUSTRATED BY HAROLD R FOSTER

Our Story : THE BODY OF KING CIDWIC IS CARRIED UP TO THE GATES OF HIS STRONG-HOLD AND A HERALD ANNOUNCES: "KING ARTHUR HAS DECLARED A TRUCE FOR TWENTY-FOUR HOURS SO YOU MAY CARE FOR YOUR WOUNDED AND BURY THE DEAD."

WITH THEIR LEADER KILLED AND THE ARMY SCATTERED, THE STRONGHOLD WISELY SURREN-DERS, AND KING ARTHUR ENTERS IN TRIUMPH.

EVEN DEFEAT CANNOT HALT THE RULE OF SUCCESSION, AND CUDDOCK, TWELVE-YEAR-OLD SON OF CIDWIC, IS CROWNED KING OF NORTH WALES.

THEN THE NEW KING IS FORGOTTEN IN THE SERIOUS BUSINESS OF TREATY MAKING.
HE IS BEFRIENDED BY ONE OF THE VETERANS OF THE LATE WAR, AND A FRIENDSHIP DEVELOPS.

KING ARTHUR IS TRYING TO SOLVE THE KNOTTY PROBLEM OF FINDING A REGENT AND SECURING THE FIDELITY OF NORTH WALES, WHEN HE SEES THE TWO BOYS RIDING OUT TOGETHER FOR A DAY OF SPORT.

1366.

"HOLD," HE SAYS, "MAYBE THAT FRIEND-SHIP WILL PROVE A STRONGER BOND THAN AN OATH OF FEALTY SWORN UNDER THE THREAT OF FORCE."

4-14-63

RUDDAH IS THE YOUNGER BROTHER OF CIDWIC AND, WITH THE DEATH OF THAT KING, HE IS ONE STEP NEARER THE THRONE. NOW ONLY THE BOY KING, CUDDOCK, STANDS IN HIS WAY TO THE POWER HE HUNGERS FOR.
NEXT WEEK- **The Stolen Arrows**

Our Story: TWO BOYS RETURN HOME FROM A DAY OF HUNTING. ONE, PRINCE ARN, THE OTHER THE NEWLY-CROWNED KING OF NORTH WALES. BUT TITLES ARE FORGOTTEN. FORGOTTEN ALSO IS THAT ONLY YESTERDAY THEY WERE ENEMIES.

TOO BAD THAT THIS HAPPY YOUNG KING MUST DIE. BUT THEN HE STANDS IN THE WAY OF HIS UNCLE RUDDAH, WHOSE INSANE DESIRE FOR POWER WILL JUSTIFY ANY CRIME.

THE SIGHT OF ARN'S QUIVER GIVES HIM A PRICELESS IDEA. FOR ARN HAS ALWAYS HAD A KEEN INTEREST IN HUNTING, AND HIS ARROWS ARE DISTINCTIVE, STRAIGHT AND TRUE WITH A RED COCK-FEATHER AND A BLUE BAND.

NOW RUDDAH, SUBTLE AS AN ADDER, PUTS HIS PLAN TO ACTION. "YOU LADS SEEM TO LIKE A WOMAN'S SPORT, ONE IN WHICH THE HAWKS DO ALL THE WORK. MUCH LIKE THE STUPID DEER HUNTERS WHOSE STAG HOUNDS FIND THE HART AND BRING IT TO BAY SO THAT IT CAN EASILY BE SLAIN."

"ONLY THE REAL SPORTSMAN HUNTS THE LOWLY RABBIT. FOR THAT TAKES CRAFT, THE SILENT STALK, THE PATIENT WAITING AND THE TRUE FLIGHT OF THE ARROW. DOWN IN THAT HOLLOW IS A WARREN WHERE I TEST MY SKILL. BUT THEN IT IS NO SPORT FOR UNTRAINED BOYS."

NATURALLY THE BOYS ACCEPT HIS CHALLENGE. IN THE MORNING THEY WILL DEMONSTRATE THEIR SKILL ON RABBITS!

RUDDAH SPREADS SUSPICION: "I DO NOT TRUST THIS ARN. HIS FATHER AND THE FATHER OF THE YOUNG KING WERE ENEMIES AND FOUGHT EACH OTHER. AND ARN MAY SEEK VENGEANCE ON THE KING."

AT DAWN RUDDAH, ARMED WITH ARN'S ARROWS, AWAITS THE COMING OF THE TWO LADS.
NEXT WEEK- **When to kick a King**

1367.

4-21-63

Prince Valiant
IN THE DAYS OF KING ARTHUR
WRITTEN AND ILLUSTRATED BY Harold R Foster

Our Story: THE RABBIT WARREN IS JUST WHERE RUDDAH HAD TOLD THEM. CIRCLING DOWN WIND THEY APPROACH CAUTIOUSLY THROUGH DENSE BRUSH.

RUDDAH LEAVES HIS LOOKOUT AND STALKS HIS PREY. THAT HE IS ABOUT TO MURDER HIS NEPHEW, WHO IS ALSO HIS KING, DOES NOT BOTHER HIM IN THE LEAST, SO GREAT IS HIS DESIRE FOR POWER.

ARN NOCKS AN ARROW IN READINESS AND MOTIONS CUDDOCK TO SILENCE . . . . . A SILENCE BROKEN BY THE SNAPPING OF A TWIG BEHIND THEM.

ARN TURNS SLOWLY BUT STILL IN TIME TO SEE A HAND HOLDING A BOW AND AN ARROW BEING DRAWN TO THE FULL.

HE LEAPS BACK AND AT THE SAME TIME DELIVERS A SWIFT KICK TO THE YOUNG KING. AN ARROW THUDS INTO A TREE WHERE CUDDOCK WAS STANDING JUST A MOMENT BEFORE!

THERE COMES THE SOUND OF THEIR ASSAIL-ANT CRASHING AWAY THROUGH THE BRUSH, AND ARN SENDS AN ARROW WHISTLING TOWARD THE SOUND.

1368.

"LOOK, ARN, ISN'T THAT ONE OF YOUR ARROWS?" AND CUDDOCK POINTS TO THE SHAFT STILL QUIVERING IN THE TREE TRUNK. ARN COUNTS HIS ARROWS.

4-28-63

"SOMEONE HAS STOLEN MY ARROWS. THREE ARE STILL MISSING. FIND WHO HAS THOSE ARROWS, AND WE WILL FIND THE ASSASSIN!"

NEXT WEEK - The Accusing Arrows

Our Story: ONE OF ARN'S MISSING ARROWS STILL QUIVERS IN THE TREE WHERE, A MOMENT BEFORE, THE YOUNG KING CUDDOCK WAS STANDING. *"HAD THAT ARROW FOUND ITS MARK, I WOULD HAVE BEEN ACCUSED OF YOUR MURDER,"* SAYS ARN.

CAUTIOUSLY THE TWO BOYS LEAVE THE WOODS, EXPECTING FURTHER ATTACK BY THE UNSEEN ASSASSIN.

BUT THE ASSASSIN HAS TROUBLES OF HIS OWN. THE ARROW ARN SHOT BLINDLY AT THE MOVEMENT IN THE THICKET PROTRUDES FROM RUDDAH'S SIDE. HE REACHES FOR THE SHAFT AND, TO HIS HORROR, IT MOVES EASILY IN HIS FINGERS.

FOR THE HEAD OF A HUNTING ARROW IS FAST TO THE SHAFT AND CAN BE WITHDRAWN, BUT A WAR ARROW IS TIPPED WITH A BOLT THAT STAYS IN THE WOUND. THERE IS BUT ONE THING TO DO. RUDDAH BACKS AGAINST A ROCK AND PUSHES THE ARROW THROUGH, REMOVES THE BOLT, AND WITHDRAWS THE SHAFT.

"YOUR LIFE IS NOT SAFE UNTIL THE ASSASSIN IS FOUND!" EXCLAIMS ARN. *"I WILL SEEK COUNCIL WITH MY FATHER."*
"AND I WILL GO TO MY UNCLE RUDDAH AND SEEK HIS AID," ANSWERS CUDDOCK.

"THE ASSAILANT STILL HAS YOUR MISSING ARROWS," SAYS VAL. *"THEY WILL PROVE HIS GUILT."*

1369.

"MY UNCLE RUDDAH HAD A HUNTING ACCIDENT AND LIES WOUNDED, BUT...." AND THE YOUNG KING HESITATES, *"I FOUND ARROWS OF YOURS IN HIS QUIVER."*

THE EVIDENCE IS ENOUGH TO CALL A MEETING OF THE COURT. THREE KNIGHTS ARE SENT TO BRING RUDDAH TO STAND TRIAL.

NEXT WEEK— **The Hunt.**

HAL FOSTER

5-5-63

Our Story: THREE KNIGHTS ARE SENT TO BRING RUDDAH TO TRIAL FOR THE ATTEMPTED ASSASSINATION OF THE YOUNG KING. BUT THE GUILTY ONE HAS FLOWN, AND THE COURT PHYSICIAN EXPLAINS: *"I WAS CALLED TO DRESS HIS WOUND, BUT HE HAS DISAPPEARED!"*

HIS OWN CLEVERNESS IS HIS UNDOING. RUDDAH USED PRINCE ARN'S ARROWS IN HIS ATTEMPT TO KILL THE KING, AND NOW POSSESSION OF THOSE ARROWS WILL CONVICT HIM. THE ARROWS MUST BE DESTROYED!

HE STAGGERS TO THE SPORT-HALL BUT FINDS HIS QUIVER EMPTY. THOSE CURSED ARROWS WITH THE RED COCK FEATHER AND THE BLUE BAND, THAT WERE TO PUT THE BLAME ON ARN, ARE GONE!

HE WHO PLOTS AGAINST A KING IS DOOMED TO A VERY UNPLEASANT DEATH. RUDDAH TAKES HORSE AND FLEES.

THERE IS BUT ONE COURSE OPEN TO RUDDAH, TO GATHER A BAND OF DISCONTENTED NOBLES AND REVOLT. HE MUST BE BROUGHT TO TRIAL IMMEDIATELY.

"I DEMAND THIS MISSION," CRIES ARN STOUTLY, *"FOR HAD RUDDAH ACHIEVED HIS PURPOSE, IT IS MY HONOR THAT WOULD HAVE BEEN FOREVER QUESTIONED!"*

1370.

SO FIRM IS HE IN HIS RESOLVE THAT HE IS GRANTED TWO MEN-AT-ARMS AND GIVEN THE KING'S WARRANT.

5-12-63

HE AND HIS MEN RIDE IN A WIDE CIRCLE, QUESTIONING THE PEASANTS UNTIL THEY FIND ONE WHO SAW RUDDAH PASS...... ON A ROAD THAT LEADS TO THE SEA.

NEXT WEEK- **Haunted Arrows.**

Prince Valiant
IN THE DAYS OF KING ARTHUR
WRITTEN AND ILLUSTRATED BY HAROLD R FOSTER

Our Story: PRINCE ARN WITH TWO WARRIORS STARTS OUT IN PURSUIT OF RUDDAH, THAT RUTHLESS ASSASSIN WHO TRIED TO WIN A CROWN BY MURDERING HIS OWN KIN AND PLACING THE BLAME ON ARN.

DAY IS ENDING AND RUDDAH MUST REST, FOR THE WOUND IN HIS SIDE IS THROBBING AND SHOULD BE CLEANSED AND DRESSED.

FROM FAR UP THE VALLEY ARN SEES HIS QUARRY DISMOUNT. UNAWARE OF PURSUIT RUDDAH PREPARES TO REST.

"MY BOW WILL NOT SEND AN ARROW THAT FAR, BUT SEE IF YOUR HEAVIER WEAPON WILL LAND A SHAFT NEAR HIM," SAYS ARN.

RUDDAH IS AROUSED BY THE THUD OF AN ARROW. HE STARES AT IT WILDLY; RED COCK FEATHER AND BLUE BAND! THOSE ACCURSED ARROWS ARE BEGINNING TO HAUNT HIM; A SYMBOL OF HIS GUILT AND DOOM.

WEARILY HE MOUNTS HIS TIRED HORSE AND LETS IT STUMBLE THROUGH THE NIGHT.

ARN AND HIS MEN RESUME THE CHASE AT THE FIRST HINT OF DAWN. THEY DO NOT KNOW HOW SERIOUS IS HIS WOUND, BUT THEY DO KNOW HIS PROWESS AS A SWORDSMAN. HE WILL BE GIVEN NO REST UNTIL EXHAUSTED

NEXT WEEK- **Down to the Sea.**

1371.

5-19-63

Our Story: FOR THE FIRST TIME IN HIS YOUNG LIFE PRINCE ARN KNOWS HATE. THE FUGITIVE, RUDDAH, IS ALL THAT HE HAS BEEN TAUGHT TO DESPISE; RUTHLESS, CRUEL, TREACHEROUS, AND HE WOULD HAVE SACRIFICED ARN TO HIS AMBITIONS.

ALL DAY THEY HAVE KEPT THEIR WEARY QUARRY IN SIGHT, AND WHEN DARKNESS FALLS ARN CREEPS DOWN TO THE CLUMP OF TREES WHERE HE WAS LAST SEEN.

AS RUDDAH AWAKENS FROM A FITFUL SLEEP THE FIRST THING HE SEES IS AN ARROW WITH BLUE BAND AND RED COCK FEATHER. HALF IN RAGE, HALF IN PANIC, HE CRUSHES THE HAUNTING SYMBOL UNDER HIS HEEL.

EVEN HIS PANIC CANNOT SPEED THE WEARY MOUNT. HE COMES TO A RIVER; A RIVER RUNS TO THE SEA, AT THE SEA THERE MUST BE BOATS, AND ESCAPE!

FROM A HILLTOP ARN LOOKS DOWN UPON THE SPARKLING SEA. ON THE SAND WHERE THE RIVER MEETS THE SEA A BOAT IS DRAWN UP, AND TOWARD THAT BOAT RUDDAH IS MAKING HIS WAY.

ARN FORGETS THAT HE HAS TWO MEN-AT-ARMS TO AID HIM. FOR THIS IS A PERSONAL MATTER BETWEEN HIM AND RUDDAH......

.....AND RUDDAH REACHES THE BOAT FIRST. "LAUNCH YOUR BOAT, CHURL," HE COMMANDS, "AND TAKE ME ACROSS THE RIVER, QUICKLY!"
NEXT WEEK- Against the Tide

1372

5-26-63

Prince Valiant
IN THE DAYS OF KING ARTHUR
WRITTEN AND ILLUSTRATED BY HAROLD R FOSTER

Our Story: WHEN PRINCE ARN SEES HIS QUARRY ESCAPING HE SPURS HIS HORSE DOWN THE SLOPE WITH RECKLESS DISREGARD FOR BROKEN BONES, LEAVING THE TWO MEN-AT-ARMS FAR BEHIND.

RUDDAH HAS REACHED THE FISHERMAN. "*LAUNCH YOUR BOAT, CHURL, AND TAKE ME ACROSS THE RIVER,*" HE COMMANDS. THE MAN LOOKS UP IN FEAR. "*WE CANNOT CROSS, SIRE, THE CURRENT IS TOO SWIFT!*"

BUT RUDDAH, HIS FACE WHITE WITH PAIN AND PANIC, WILL BROOK NO DENIAL. HE DRAWS HIS SWORD. "*BUT LOOK, SIRE,*" SCREAMS THE MAN, "*WHERE THE OUTFLOWING RIVER MEETS THE INCOMING TIDE THERE IS CERTAIN DEATH!*"

IN BLIND RAGE HE CUTS THE MAN DOWN, ENTERS THE CORACLE, AND WITH HIS ONE GOOD ARM PUSHES OFF INTO THE CURRENT. NO LONGER CAN RUDDAH HAVE HIS COMMANDS OBEYED. LIKE ANY OTHER PIECE OF FLOTSAM HE IS SWEPT TOWARD THE AWFUL TURMOIL WHERE RIVER AND SEA CONTEND.

AS THE RAGING WATERS TEAR THE FRAIL BOAT APART HE LOOKS BACK FOR A GLIMPSE OF HIS DETERMINED PURSUERS. AND RUDDAH, WHO WAS BUT ONE STEP FROM BECOMING KING, SEES A SMALL BOY STANDING AT THE WATER'S EDGE.

1373.

WHEN THE LAST BIT OF WRECKAGE HAS DISAPPEARED ARN TURNS BACK TO HIS HORSE AND THE WATCHER ON THE HILL ALSO TURNS HOMEWARD.

NEXT WEEK- **The Watcher**

6-2-63

Prince Valiant

IN THE DAYS OF KING ARTHUR

WRITTEN AND ILLUSTRATED BY Harold R. Foster

Our Story: RUDDAH IS DEAD AND NORTH WALES SAVED FROM A RUINOUS STRUGGLE FOR POWER. PRINCE ARN HAS ACCOMPLISHED HIS MISSION. HE FEELS NO GREAT JOY IN HIS SUCCESS. HE WISHES ONLY THAT HIS MOTHER WERE NEAR.

THE WATCHER ON A DISTANT HILLSIDE TURNS HIS HORSE HOMEWARD. HE HAS NEVER BEEN FAR AWAY SINCE THE HUNT BEGAN.

VAL SINGS AS HE RIDES, FOR HE HAS SEEN HIS STURDY SON COMPLETE WITH COURAGE AND WISDOM THE MISSION FOR WHICH HE VOLUNTEERED.

ARN MAKES A FORMAL REPORT BEFORE THE YOUNG KING CUDDOCK, AND ARTHUR SMILES AS HE REMEMBERS ANOTHER SUCH LAD. PRINCE VALIANT WAS ABOUT THIS AGE WHEN HE FIRST CAME TO CAMELOT.

FROM A WINDY HILLTOP THE TWO FRIENDS WATCH KING ARTHUR LEAD HIS KNIGHTS ON THE LONG ROAD BACK TO CAMELOT. PRINCE VALIANT AND ARN HAVE BEEN LEFT BEHIND TO ATTEND TO SOME MATTERS OF ADMINISTRATION.

FOR ARTHUR HOPES THAT A WARM FRIENDSHIP BETWEEN ARN AND YOUNG KING CUDDOCK WILL BE MORE BINDING THAN A TREATY.

1374.

HAL FOSTER

WHEN AT LAST FATHER AND SON RIDE HOMEWARD IT IS THE SEASON OF PENTECOST. THE HARVESTS ARE IN, WORK FOR THE YEAR ENDED, AND IT IS TIME TO CELEBRATE WITH TOURNAMENT AND BANQUET. MANY KNIGHTS ARE TRAVELING THE ROADS.

NEXT WEEK- The Tour

6-9-63

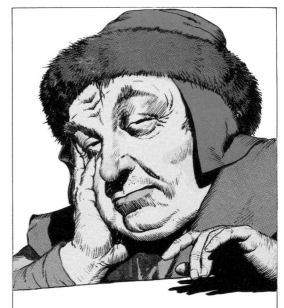

Our Story: PRINCE VALIANT AND ARN BEGIN THEIR LONG JOURNEY BACK TO CAMELOT THROUGH THE BRIGHT AUTUMN WOODS. MANY KNIGHTS ARE ON THE ROAD, FOR THIS IS THAT TIME OF YEAR BETWEEN HARVEST AND WINTER, WHEN EACH CASTLE MAKES MERRY WITH BANQUET AND TOURNAMENT.

IT IS A HOLIDAY FOR EVERYONE BUT THE LORD OF THE CASTLE. CUSTOM DEMANDS THAT HE FURNISH LODGINGS FOR HIS GUESTS, FOOD AND ENTERTAINMENT FOR VASSALS, VILLEINS AND SERFS, AND A SUITABLE PURSE FOR THE VICTORS. HIS HARVEST WILL HARDLY LAST UNTIL WINTER.

THE LIVING QUARTERS IN THE KEEP CONSIST OF TWO LARGE ROOMS. THE INVITED MEN ENJOY THE LUXURY OF THE MAIN HALL AND ARE PROVIDED WITH FRESH RUSHES ON THE FLOOR. THEIR LADIES ARE MADE JUST AS COMFORTABLE IN THE SLEEPING ROOM ABOVE.

THE YOUNG KNIGHTS WHO ARE MAKING "THE TOUR" OF THE JOUSTS TO WIN FAME OR A RICH WIFE, MERELY HOPE FOR A WARM, DRY NIGHT AND SLEEP WHERE THEY CAN.

PRINCE VALIANT IS THE MOST HONORED GUEST, FOR, OF ALL THE KNIGHTS IN BRITAIN, ONLY NINETY-NINE ARE CHOSEN FOR THE FELLOWSHIP OF THE ROUND TABLE. THE ONE HUNDREDTH SEAT, "THE SIEGE PERILOUS", HAS NOT YET BEEN FILLED.

1375.

AT DAWN THE FUN BEGINS. ARCHERS, WRESTLERS AND KNIGHTS CONTEND. JUGGLERS, ACROBATS AND JONGLEURS ADD TO THE CONFUSION, AND THE STABLES ARE TURNED INTO A HOSPITAL. MARSHALS, UMPIRES AND JUDGES SHOUT AND SCREAM AS THEY TRY TO DECLARE THE WINNERS.

NEXT WEEK- **The Rustic Knights**

6-16-63

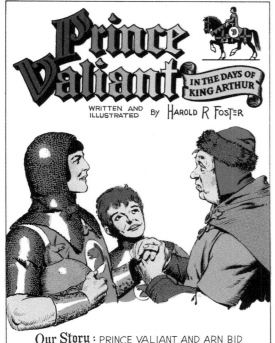

Prince Valiant
IN THE DAYS OF KING ARTHUR
WRITTEN AND ILLUSTRATED BY HAROLD R FOSTER

Our Story : PRINCE VALIANT AND ARN BID FAREWELL TO THEIR HOST AND LEAVE HIM TO CONTEMPLATE AN EMPTY LARDER AND THE WRECKAGE LEFT BY THE TOURNAMENT.

'THE TOUR' MOVES SOUTHWARD FROM ONE TOURNAMENT TO ANOTHER, EACH YOUNG KNIGHT HOPING TO SURVIVE UNTIL THE END OF PENTECOST AND ENTER THE CHAMPIONSHIPS AT CAMELOT.

BY CUSTOM, THE HORSE AND ARMOR OF A DEFEATED KNIGHT BELONG TO THE VICTOR, TO BE REDEEMED AT A PRICE.

TWO RUSTIC KNIGHTS, BOSWELL FARNWAY, KNOWN AS 'BO,' AND HIS LIFELONG FRIEND CHETWORTH DILLINGFORD, CALLED 'CHET,' EXPERIENCE THE FORTUNES OF WAR. FOR BO HAS WON CHET'S HORSE AND ARMOR, AND CHET HAS NO MONEY TO REDEEM THEM.

AT THE NEXT TOURNAMENT CHET MAKES A PLEA: "LOAN ME MY ARMOR AND I WILL CHALLENGE SIR PLUMPET TO A JOUST. I CANNOT LOSE, FOR PLUMPET CAROUSED LAST NIGHT AND CAN HARDLY SIT A HORSE."

BO SUCCUMBS TO CHET'S ELOQUENCE AND GRUDGINGLY ALLOWS HIM TO DON THE ARMOR.
BUT EITHER SIR PLUMPET HAS EXCEPTIONAL LUCK OR THEY HAVE MISJUDGED HIS CAPACITY. CHET IS TUMBLED AND LOSES HORSE AND ARMOR.

THE INCIDENT IS A GREAT STRAIN ON THEIR FRIENDSHIP. BO IS NOT TOO MUCH OF AN ORATOR, BUT WHAT HE DOES SAY IS BOTH LOUD AND TO THE POINT.
NEXT WEEK— **Knight in the night**

1376.
6-23-63

Prince Valiant
IN THE DAYS OF KING ARTHUR
WRITTEN AND ILLUSTRATED BY HAROLD R FOSTER

Our Story: PRINCE VALIANT AND ARN JOURNEY SOUTHWARD WITH THE TROOP OF KNIGHTS WHO ARE MAKING A TOUR OF THE AUTUMN TOURNAMENTS IN THE HOPE OF WINNING FAME AND FORTUNE.

AND FORTUNE HAS NOT SMILED ON CHET. HE HAS JOUSTED WITH SIR PLUMPET AND LOST HIS HORSE AND ARMOR. HE FOLLOWS THE TOUR AFOOT IN THE HOPE OF REDEEMING HIS ARMS OR FINDING A SPONSOR.

AT LAST THE TAUNTS OF HIS FRIEND BO ARE TOO, TOO MUCH AND HE LOSES HIS TEMPER. "YAP, YAP, YAP!" HE SHOUTS, "IF YOU THINK YOU CAN DO BETTER, YOU WINDY BAGPIPE, YOU CHALLENGE SIR PLUMPET, THERE HE LIES TOO DRUNK TO SIT A HORSE!"

IT IS EVEN AS CHET SAID. THE DOUGHTY OLD KNIGHT LOOKS FAR FROM DANGEROUS, SO BO CHALLENGES HIM TO A JOUST.

BUT ONCE AGAIN SIR PLUMPET MAKES A MIRACULOUS RECOVERY. BO IS PLUCKED FROM HIS SADDLE, AND THE VICTOR ADDS HIS HORSE AND ARMOR TO HIS MOUNTING COLLECTION.

TWO RUSTIC KNIGHTS WATCH THE TOURNAMENT WITHOUT MUCH INTEREST. ALL THEY POSSESSED IN THE WORLD WAS THE JOUSTING EQUIPMENT THEY HAVE LOST.

SIR CHET IS ALSO IN DEBT TO SIR BO, AND HIS CONDITION IS DESPERATE. FROM A NEARBY HEDGE HE CUTS A CROOK.....

1377.

.....AND, IN THE DARK NIGHT, CREEPS UNDER THE EDGE OF SIR PLUMPET'S PATCHED PAVILION.
NEXT WEEK- Skulduggery

6-30-63

Prince Valiant
IN THE DAYS OF KING ARTHUR
WRITTEN AND ILLUSTRATED BY HAROLD R FOSTER

Our Story TELLS HOW THE TWO RUSTIC KNIGHTS, BO AND CHET, MET MISFORTUNE DURING A TOURNAMENT AND LOST HORSE AND ARMS TO DOUGHTY SIR PLUMPET.

BUT CHET GOES TO SIR PLUMPET'S TENT IN THE DARK OF NIGHT AND, WITH A CROOKED STICK, RETRIEVES HIS SHIELD, SADDLE, HELM AND SHIRT OF MAIL. AS AN AFTERTHOUGHT HE ALSO HOOKS THE OLD KNIGHT'S WINE JUG.

WHILE CHANGING THE COLOR OF HELM AND SHIELD CHET TAKES A PULL AT THE JUG..... WATER! SIR PLUMPET IS NOT THE DRUNKEN SOT HE PRETENDS TO BE IN ORDER TO GET MATCHES WITH LESSER KNIGHTS; THE CROOK!

CHET IS SO ENRAGED AT THIS DISHONESTY THAT HE STEALS A HORSE AND WAITS HIDDEN IN THE FOREST FOR THE TOURNAMENT TO BEGIN.

BUT SIR BO HAS ALSO GONE PROWLING THIS NIGHT. HE HAS SEEN CHET RETRIEVE HIS LOST ARMOR, SO, PULLING A SACK OVER SIR PLUMPET'S SLEEPING HEAD, HE TRUSSES HIM UP AND BORROWS HIS ARMOR.

BY THE LUCK OF THE DRAW THE TWO FRIENDS MEET IN THE TRIAL ROUND, AND THOUGH EACH MISSES THE OTHER, THEIR LANCES TANGLE AND BOTH ARE UNSEATED. THE CRASH OF THEIR FALLING IS DROWNED IN A LOUDER NOISE......

HAL FOSTER

....SIR PLUMPET HAS AT LAST FREED HIM-SELF AND IS SCREAMING FOR JUSTICE. HE CALLS HIS HOST, THE MARSHALS, REFEREES AND UMPIRES FOR REDRESS.

NEXT WEEK-**Rags to Riches and Back**

7-7-63

1378

Prince Valiant

IN THE DAYS OF KING ARTHUR

WRITTEN AND ILLUSTRATED HAROLD R FOSTER

Our Story: SIR PLUMPET GALLOPS OUT ONTO THE FIELD BELLOWING THAT THE TWO FALLEN KNIGHTS ARE USING HORSES AND ARMS THAT HAVE BEEN STOLEN FROM HIM.

THE EVIDENCE IS CONCLUSIVE AND THE MARSHALS DECREE THAT CHET AND BO BECOME SERVANTS OF SIR PLUMPET UNTIL THEY HAVE WORKED OUT THE PRICE THAT WILL REDEEM THEIR ARMS.

SIR PLUMPET, A VETERAN OF THE SMALL TOURNAMENTS, HAS NEVER FELT SO IMPORTANT. HE HAS TWO RETAINERS WHO COOK, SET UP HIS TENT, TEND THE HORSES, AND SERVE HIM LIKE A GREAT LORD.

AS THEY MOVE SOUTHWARD THE TOURNAMENTS BECOME BIGGER, THE PRIZES RICHER, AND THE QUALITY OF THE KNIGHTS BETTER. STILL, SIR PLUMPET FEELS THEIR EQUAL. SO HE ISSUES A CHALLENGE TO SINGLE COMBAT.... AND LOSES.

HE ALSO LOSES HIS TEMPER AND ISSUES CHALLENGES RIGHT AND LEFT. AT DAY'S END SIR CHET AND SIR BO DRAG THEIR BATTERED MASTER FROM THE LISTS.

WHILE PLAYING THE PART OF A BESOTTED OLD MAN HE WON MUCH RUSTY AND DENTED ARMOR AND SPAVINED HORSES. NOW NOTHING REMAINS BUT HIS PATCHED TENT AND TWO HUNGRY SQUIRES.

1379.

WHILE TRAVELING SOUTH WITH THE TOURING KNIGHTS, VAL AND ARN HAVE BEEN AMUSED AT THE CHANGING FORTUNES OF THESE THREE RUSTIC WARRIORS. AND UNLESS THEIR FORTUNES CHANGE FOR THE BETTER THEY WILL HAVE A LONG WALK BACK TO THEIR HOMES.

NEXT WEEK- **The Bargain**

HAL FOSTER

7-14-63

Prince Valiant
IN THE DAYS OF KING ARTHUR
WRITTEN AND ILLUSTRATED BY HAROLD R FOSTER

Our Story HAS TOLD OF THE CHANGING FORTUNES (ALWAYS FOR THE WORSE) OF THREE RUSTIC KNIGHTS: SIRS PLUMPET, CHET AND BO. PLUMPET HAS LOST EVERYTHING BUT A TORN AND PATCHED PAVILION, WHILE CHET AND BO ARE IN DEBT TO HIM AND MUST SERVE HIM UNTIL THEIR DEBT IS DISCHARGED.

PRINCE VALIANT OFFERS A SOLUTION: "MY SON AND I WISH TO FINISH OUR JOURNEY TO CAMELOT IN COMFORT. I WILL BUY YOUR TENT AND THE DEBTS OF SIR CHETWORTH AND SIR BOSWELL."

SIR PLUMPET IS BELLOWING A SONG AS HE SETS OUT ON THE LONG WALK BACK TO HIS FARM. HAPPILY HE JINGLES THE COINS IN HIS PURSE. IT IS NOT MUCH, BUT MORE THAN HE HAS EVER HAD ALL AT ONE TIME.

"THERE GOES OLD PLUMPET. WE ARE FREE AGAIN, FREE!" CRIES THE OVERLY OPTIMISTIC CHET.
"YOU WILL BE FREE WHEN YOU HAVE WORKED OUT THE DEBT YOU NOW OWE ME," ANSWERS VAL STERNLY. "NOW ROLL UP THE TENT AND SADDLE OUR HORSES!"

WINTER, AS IF ASHAMED OF BEING SO MILD, TURNS ON THE RAIN AND SLEET. VAL AND ARN DECIDE TO RIDE STRAIGHT TO CAMELOT

A TENT, EVEN A PATCHED AND LEAKY ONE, IS A GREAT COMFORT.
"IF WE 'BORROW' THEIR HORSES AND ARMOR WE CAN ENTER THE NEXT TOURNAMENT AND WIN FAME AND GLORY," WHISPERS CHET.
"SHUT UP," ANSWERS BO.

1380.

BUT AS THEY PASS KING KADONOC'S CASTLE THE WEATHER IS SO BRIGHT AND CRISP VAL'S PLANS ARE CHANGED. THEY WILL TAKE IN ONE MORE TOURNAMENT.
NEXT WEEK- The Challenge

7-21-63

Our Story: ARN IS EAGER TO SEE ANOTHER TOURNAMENT AND PRINCE VALIANT IS EASILY PERSUADED, FOR THIS IS A BIG TOURNAMENT. MANY FAMOUS KNIGHTS WILL CONTEND AND VAL FEELS HE SHOULD HAVE SOME PRACTICE.

A TOURNAMENT IS NOT ONLY A WAR GAME; IT IS A COUNTRY FAIR, CIRCUS, MARKET, AND ENDLESS NOISE AND CONFUSION. VAL BUYS A TILTING HELM.

AMONG THE BRIGHT PAVILIONS, CHET AND BO SET UP THE PATCHED AND TORN TENT. THE JOKING AND TAUNTS CEASE WHEN CHET HANGS VAL'S SHIELD BEFORE THE DOOR, FOR IT IS KNOWN THAT ILL HEALTH FOLLOWS QUICKLY ANYONE WHO JEERS AT THE WEARER OF THE CRIMSON STALLION.

THE PRELIMINARIES HAVE BEEN DECIDED AND THE MAIN EVENTS BEGIN WITH MUCH POMP AND CEREMONY. FIRST THE GRAND MELEE; THE CONTESTANTS FORM TWO EQUAL LINES, AND THE MARSHAL, WITH A WAVE OF HIS BATON, SENDS THEM THUNDERING TOGETHER.

LANCES ARE SHATTERED, HORSES AND KNIGHTS GO DOWN IN SATISFACTORY CONFUSION. NO EDGED WEAPONS ARE ALLOWED IN THE MELEE, BUT WOODEN TRUNCHEONS MAKE BEAUTIFUL MUSIC ON IRON HELMS.

THE HORSE AND ARMOR OF A DEFEATED KNIGHT ARE NOT FORFEIT TO THE VICTOR, BECAUSE WHO CAN TELL WHO UNHORSED WHOM? THE VICTORIOUS KNIGHTS LINE UP FOR THE CHALLENGE ROUND.

1381.

RORY MAC AIN, A YOUNG IRISH KNIGHT, HAS WON MOST OF THE MINOR TOURNAMENTS. NOW HE MUST PUT HIS SKILL TO THE TEST.

HE RIDES UP TO PRINCE VALIANT AND TOUCHES HIS SHIELD WITH HIS LANCE. A CHALLENGE TO SINGLE COMBAT HAS BEEN GIVEN.
NEXT WEEK-**A False Knight**

7-28-63

Prince Valiant
IN THE DAYS OF KING ARTHUR
WRITTEN AND ILLUSTRATED BY Harold R Foster

Our Story : PRINCE VALIANT CALLS TO HIS SQUIRES TO ARM HIM FOR THE CONTEST, FOR HE HAS BEEN CHALLENGED TO A TILT WITH......

....RORY MAC AIN, A YOUNG IRISH KNIGHT WHO HAS DONE WELL IN THE TOURNAMENTS, BUT IS EAGER TO TEST HIS HARDIHOOD AGAINST A ROUND-TABLE KNIGHT.

SIR CHET AND SIR BO, NOW REDUCED TO THE RANK OF SQUIRE, WATCH EAGERLY AS THEIR MASTER AND RORY SHATTER THEIR LANCES BUT HOLD FIRM IN THEIR SADDLES.

TO FIGHT A DRAW WITH SUCH A CELEBRATED KNIGHT AS PRINCE VALIANT WOULD HAVE BROUGHT FAME TO RORY, BUT HE IS IRISH, AND EAGERNESS FOR COMBAT OVERCOMES HIS JUDGMENT. HE HAS CHALLENGED FOR THREE COURSES. ON THE SECOND HE IS UNHORSED

HARDLY HAS RORY HIT THE TURF WHEN, LIKE A PAIR OF HARPIES, CHET AND BO ARE UPON HIM, STRIPPING HIM OF HIS ARMOR.

THE ARMOR IS FORFEIT TO VAL, BUT THE GREED OF HIS SQUIRES IS A REFLECTION ON HIS COURTESY. VAL SEEKS OUT RORY TO APOLOGIZE. RORY IS ANGRY: "*HERE IS MY PURSE. I WISH TO REDEEM MY HARNESS!*"

"*YOU ARE A DARING LAD; THE ARMOR IS YOURS WITHOUT FEE,*" SAYS VAL. BUT IT HAS DISAPPEARED! UNDER QUESTIONING, BO POINTS SHEEPISHLY.....

1382.

HAL FOSTER

.....AND THERE, IN THE CHALLENGE LINE, MOUNTED ON RORY'S HORSE AND WEARING HIS ARMOR, IS SIR CHET!

NEXT WEEK- **The Village Champion**

8-4-63

Our Story: ONCE AGAIN SIR CHET 'BORROWS' A SUIT OF ARMOR AND TAKES HIS PLACE IN THE CHALLENGE LINE, WHERE HE DEFINITELY DOES NOT BELONG.

THE MARSHALS DISCOVER THE 'RINGER', BUT BEFORE THEY CAN DO ANYTHING PRINCE VALIANT LEAPS INTO THE SADDLE AND GALLOPS OUT ONTO THE FIELD.

CHET SEES VAL COMING DIRECTLY TOWARD HIM AND SHUDDERS. "THIS IS UNFAIR," HE MUTTERS, "A ROUND-TABLE KNIGHT SHOULD WAIT MODESTLY TO BE CHALLENGED, SO HE NOT BE ACCUSED OF PICKING AN EASY OPPONENT."

"BUT MAYHAP I WILL WIN, FOR AM I NOT THE GREATEST WARRIOR OF MY VILLAGE?" HE FORGETS THAT HE HAS LOST EVERY JOUST SINCE THE TOURNAMENTS BEGAN. HE DREAMS OF WINNING THIS ONE, FOR HOPE SPRINGS ETERNAL WITH THE STUPID.

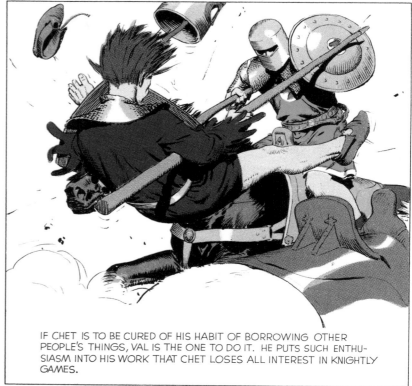

IF CHET IS TO BE CURED OF HIS HABIT OF BORROWING OTHER PEOPLE'S THINGS, VAL IS THE ONE TO DO IT. HE PUTS SUCH ENTHUSIASM INTO HIS WORK THAT CHET LOSES ALL INTEREST IN KNIGHTLY GAMES.

THE GRAND MARSHAL DECLARES CHET RECREANT AND HE IS PUT IN THE DUNGEON TO MEDITATE.

"MASTER, CHET IS MY BEST, MY ONLY FRIEND. MAY I SERVE HALF HIS SENTENCE?" VAL IS TOUCHED BY BO'S PLEA AND ARRANGES NOT ONLY CHET'S RELEASE, BUT GIVES THEM THE PACK HORSES AND SENDS THEM HOME.

WITHOUT THE ANTICS OF CHET AND BO THE TOURNAMENTS BECOME DULL. VAL AND ARN TAKE THE ROAD TO CAMELOT, EAGER NOW FOR THE WARMTH AND COMFORT OF FAMILY LIFE.

NEXT WEEK- **Homage**

8-11-63

Our Story : CAMELOT! AND AS PRINCE VALIANT AND HIS SON MOUNT THE GREAT STAIRWAY HE FEELS AGAIN THE WAVE OF PRIDE AND EXCITEMENT THAT SWEEPS OVER HIM EACH TIME HE ENTERS THIS CASTLE OF MARVEL.

THE KING IS HOLDING COURT ATTENDED BY SIR LAUNCELOT AND QUEEN GUINEVERE. SIR VALIANT AND HIS STALWART SON PAY THEIR HOMAGE.

THEN COMES A SQUEAL OF DELIGHT, A PATTER OF FEET, AND THE DIGNITY OF THE OCCASION IS RUINED AS KAREN AND VALETA GREET THEIR LONG-ABSENT SIRE.

"NEVER HAVE WE WELCOMED A FATHER WITH MORE SINCERITY. WE HAVE SCATTERED THE DANES AND CAN HOLD THE SAXONS AT BAY, BUT FROM THE EXUBERANCE OF YOUR DAUGHTERS WE HAVE NO DEFENSE."

FROM THE AUDIENCE COMES ALETA'S CALM VOICE REMINDING THE TWINS OF THEIR MANNERS. THEY CURTSY TO THE THRONE, FOR THEY HAVE LEARNED LONG SINCE THAT IN THE PRESENCE OF THEIR MOTHER IT IS WISE TO ACT LIKE LITTLE ANGELS.

1384.

SIR VALIANT IS GIVEN LEAVE TO RETIRE. FOR WELL KING ARTHUR KNOWS THAT VAL IS ANXIOUS TO BE WITH HIS FAMILY.

8-18-63

VAL IS ABOUT TO LEAD THE WAY TO THE SOUTH TOWER WHERE THEY HAD BEEN QUARTERED, WHEN ALETA TAKES HIS HAND. "COME," SHE SAYS EAGERLY, "WE HAVE A NEW HOME!" NEXT WEEK— **The New Home**

Prince Valiant
IN THE DAYS OF KING ARTHUR

WRITTEN AND ILLUSTRATED BY HAROLD R FOSTER

Our Story: ALETA LEADS PRINCE VALIANT OUT OF THE PALACE, THROUGH THE TOWN, AND ON THE OUTSKIRTS POINTS OUT THEIR NEW HOME. *"THE PALACE IS NO PLACE TO BRING UP CHILDREN. EVERYONE SPOILS THEM. AND,"* SHE ADDS, *"QUEEN GUINEVERE IS THE WORST OF ALL. SHE CAN DENY THEM NOTHING."*

SPACIOUS COURTYARD, STABLES, WELL, KITCHEN GARDEN, BUTTERY, AND ALL WITHIN THE OUTER CURTAIN WALL.

VAL SIGHS CONTENTEDLY. SO MUCH OF HIS LIFE HAS BEEN SPENT AHORSE, IN CAMPAIGNS, IN STARK FORTRESSES AND GRIM CASTLES, THAT HE HAS ALMOST FORGOTTEN THE JOYS OF A HOME.

THE STABLE IS NO PLACE TO KEEP SUCH A WAR HORSE AS ARVAK. HE IS TAKEN TO THE HORSE RUNS AND ONCE AGAIN BECOMES THE KING AND PROTECTOR OF A HERD OF BROOD MARES.

TRAINERS BRING OUT THE COLTS ARVAK HAS SIRED AND VAL SWELLS WITH PRIDE. HERE IS HIS REAL WEALTH, FOR ONLY BY BEING SUPERBLY MOUNTED CAN ARTHUR'S KNIGHTS COPE WITH THE ENCROACHING SAXON HORDES.

1385

VAL IS DELIGHTED THAT HIS OLD FRIEND SIR GAWAIN IS IN CAMELOT AND WISHES TO MEET HIM AT THE GOLDEN ROOSTER TAVERN.

VAL GREETS HIM JOYFULLY, BUT GAWAIN IS PREOCCUPIED. *"COME WITH ME. THERE IS A MEETING TAKING PLACE THAT IS OF GREAT IMPORTANCE."*

NEXT WEEK- **Seeds of Revolt**

8-25-63

HAL FOSTER

Prince Valiant
IN THE DAYS OF KING ARTHUR

WRITTEN AND ILLUSTRATED BY HAROLD R FOSTER

Our Story: A SERIOUS SIR GAWAIN OPENS A DOOR AND USHERS A VERY PUZZLED PRINCE VALIANT INTO A CROWDED ROOM, WHERE MODRED IS PRESIDING OVER A MEETING.

"THE RULES AND LAWS OF THE FELLOWSHIP OF THE TABLE ROUND MUST BE CHANGED," HE IS SAYING. "FOR EIGHTEEN YEARS WE HAVE FOUGHT. ALL THE PLUNDER GOES TO KING ARTHUR, WHILE WE HAVE ONLY OUR WOUNDS!"

"TO THE VICTOR BELONG THE SPOILS, BUT AFTER OUR VICTORIES WE REMAIN POOR KNIGHTS WITHOUT THE POWER AND THE TITLES THAT WEALTH WOULD BRING US." THERE IS A MURMUR OF APPROVAL AT THESE WORDS.

MODRED NOTES THAT VAL DOES NOT APPLAUD. "DOES NOT SIR VALIANT AGREE?"
"NO, SIR MODRED, THE KING HAS AS MANY WOUNDS AS ANY OF YOU, AND THE WEALTH SUPPORTS THE FELLOWSHIP ABUNDANTLY."

"WITHOUT THE RULES THE FELLOWSHIP WOULD BREAK UP INTO PLUNDERING BANDS, TO BE CRUSHED EACH IN TURN BY THE SAXONS. BETTER TO BE A TRUE KING'S KNIGHT THAN A SAXON SLAVE!"

1386

MODRED'S FACE SHOWS NO EMOTION, ONLY HIS EYES SHOW HIS VENOM. NO VIPER IS MORE DEADLY THAN MODRED WHEN CROSSED. HE TURNS TO GAWAIN —

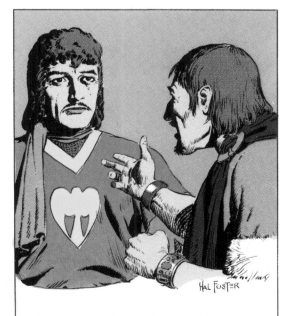

"I WARNED YOU NOT TO BRING THAT STIFF-NECKED LACKEY OF THE KING. ONLY DEATH CAN QUENCH HIS SMUG, TOP-LOFTY VIRTUE!"

NEXT WEEK— **Slow Poison**

9-1-63

Prince Valiant
IN THE DAYS OF KING ARTHUR
WRITTEN AND ILLUSTRATED BY HAROLD R FOSTER

Our Story: PRINCE VALIANT GLANCES BACK INTO THE MEETING ROOM. NO ROUND TABLE KNIGHTS ARE PRESENT, ONLY EAGER YOUTHS EASILY SWAYED BY MODRED'S CLEVERNESS.

SIR MODRED ENDS THE MEETING. HE HAD SOWN THE SEEDS OF DISCONTENT, BUT VAL'S SIMPLE, HONEST WORDS HAVE UNDONE ALL HIS EFFORTS.

ONLY THE LOTHIAN CLAN REMAINS -- THE FOUR SONS OF KING LOT: GAWAIN, GARETH, GEHERIS, AGRAVAINE; AND THEIR HALF-BROTHER, MODRED. AND MODRED, CLEVER, RUTHLESS AND AMBITIOUS, DOMINATES THE OTHERS.

"AS LONG AS LAUNCELOT STANDS AT ARTHUR'S RIGHT HAND THE KING'S POWER IS UNBREAKABLE. INSTEAD OF THE WEALTH AND POWER THAT IS OUR RIGHT, WE WILL CONTINUE TO BE THE KING'S LACKEYS WITH A DAILY PORTION OF PIETY AND GOODNESS, LIKE OBEDIENT SCHOOLBOYS."

"IT IS WELL KNOWN THAT GUINEVERE LOVES SIR LAUNCELOT. IF WE CAN AROUSE HER JEALOUSY, IT MIGHT CAUSE A RIFT. AND IF WE CAN USE PRINCE VALIANT'S WIFE IN RUMORS OF THE SCANDAL........!"

9-8-63

"NO!" THUNDERS GAWAIN, "VAL IS MY GOOD FRIEND. HURT HIM AT YOUR PERIL!" AND HE STOMPS OUT.

HE VISITS VAL BUT SITS IN WORRIED SILENCE, TORN BETWEEN STAUNCH LOYALTY TO HIS CLAN AND HIS LOVE FOR VAL AND ALETA.

NEXT WEEK-**Divided Loyalties**

Prince Valiant
IN THE DAYS OF KING ARTHUR
WRITTEN AND ILLUSTRATED BY HAROLD R FOSTER

Our Story : SIR GAWAIN SITS BROODING BEFORE PRINCE VALIANT'S FIREPLACE; A GALLANT WARRIOR, A CHARMING PLAYBOY, BUT NOT CLEVER ENOUGH TO SOLVE HIS PROBLEM..... HOW TO CHOOSE BETWEEN HIS FIERCE CLAN-LOYALTY AND HIS OATH TO HIS KING!

"YOU HAVE BEEN HERE FOR AN HOUR WITHOUT TELLING ME HOW BEAUTIFUL I AM," COMPLAINS ALETA. "AM I BECOMING UGLY, GAWAIN, OR ARE YOU WORRIED? IS IT ANYTHING YOU CAN SHARE WITH US?"

"NAH, NAH, I K'NNA BOTHER YE WI' ME TROUBLES," ANSWERS GAWAIN, FALLING INTO THE CALEDONIAN ACCENT AS HE ALWAYS DOES IN MOMENTS OF STRESS. "BUT BE ALERT FOR TROUBLES OF YOUR OWN!"

THE LOTHIAN CLAN GATHERS: GARETH, A FINE KNIGHT BUT BLINDLY DEVOTED TO HIS CLAN; GAHARIS, NOT A LEADER, BUT ONE WHO WILL FOLLOW HIS CHIEF TO THE END; AGRAVAINE, A BULLY, CRUEL AND STUPID.....

.... AND THEIR HALF-BROTHER, MODRED. MODRED SPEAKS: "WE ARE THE SONS OF KINGS WITH BETTER RIGHT TO THE THRONE THAN ARTHUR. ARTHUR AND HIS FATHER UTHER PENDRAGON HUMBLED OUR CLAN. LAUNCELOT HAS HURLED ALL OF YOU TO THE DUST IN JOUSTS. QUEEN ALETA HAS THWARTED ME ONCE!" (TO MODRED THAT IS A CRIME MERITING DESTRUCTION.)

"TOMORROW PRINCE VALIANT AND HIS FAMILY DINE WITH THE KING AND QUEEN. IF OUR PLAN WORKS IT WILL DESTROY THE UNITY OF THE FELLOWSHIP!"

1388   9-15-63

THE PRIVATE DINNER IS A GREAT SUCCESS. ALETA WATCHES WITH PRIDE AS ARN TELLS OF HIS ADVENTURES IN THE NORTH WALES CAMPAIGN, AND THE QUEEN, AS USUAL, INDULGES THE TWINS WITH TOO MANY SWEETS.

NEXT WEEK— The Plot

HAL FOSTER

Our Story: PRINCE VALIANT AND HIS FAMILY HAVE A PRIVATE DINNER WITH THE KING AND QUEEN. THEY LINGER OVER THEIR WINE, BUT THE TWINS ARE EXCUSED AND SCAMPER OUT IN THE GROWING DUSK TO FIND SOME ENTERTAINING MISCHIEF.

THEY MEET GAHARIS AND HE TELLS THEM OF THE MANY STRANGE AND INTERESTING THINGS HE HAS IN HIS ROOM. THEY BEG HIM TO SHOW THEM.

ALETA, SEARCHING FOR HER ENERGETIC DAUGHTERS, MEETS GARETH. "YES, I SAW THEM, THEY WERE HEADED FOR THE QUEEN'S GARDEN," HE STAMMERS, FOR HIS HEART IS NOT IN THIS PLOT.

AGRAVAINE SEEKS OUT SIR LAUNCELOT. "THE FAIR ALETA IS HAVING HER TROUBLES WITH THE TWINS," HE LAUGHS. "THEY ARE LOST IN THE QUEEN'S GARDEN AND SHE MUST FIND THEM BEFORE THEY CATCH COLD."

"WILL YOU JOIN ME IN THE SEARCH?" ASKS LAUNCELOT. "OH, NO," ANSWERS AGRAVAINE, "THE QUEEN IS DISPLEASED WITH ME AND WOULD NOT LIKE ME TO ENTER HER PRIVATE GARDEN."

MODRED APPEARS FROM THE DEEPENING SHADOWS AND SLYLY TURNS THE KEY.

9-22-63

LAUNCELOT MEETS ALETA AT THE PAVILION. "I CANNOT FIND THEM, THOUGH I HAVE SEARCHED EVERYWHERE," SHE COMPLAINS. "THEY ARE NOT HERE."

ON RETURNING THEY FIND THE DOOR LOCKED. EVEN LAUNCELOT'S GREAT STRENGTH CANNOT BUDGE IT.

NEXT WEEK— **The Scandal**

1389

Prince Valiant
IN THE DAYS OF KING ARTHUR
WRITTEN AND ILLUSTRATED BY HAROLD R FOSTER

Our Story: NIGHT HAS FALLEN AND THE TORCHES LIT, WHEN THE MISSING TWINS TURN UP. NOW ONLY ALETA IS UNACCOUNTED FOR. VAL IS ANXIOUS, FOR HE REMEMBERS SIR GAWAIN'S WARNING: "BE ALERT FOR TROUBLES OF YOUR OWN."

ARN TAKES HIS SISTERS HOME ON THE OFF CHANCE THAT THEIR MOTHER MIGHT HAVE RETURNED THERE. HE IS DISAPPOINTED AND RUNS BACK TO THE PALACE.....

.....IN TIME TO HEAR MODRED SAYING: "THIS KEY WILL REVEAL THAT THERE ARE MORE THAN STATUES IN THE QUEEN'S GARDEN. BE HERE AT DAWN AND BRING ALL WHO WILL COME TO WITNESS THE COMEDY."

MEANWHILE LAUNCELOT AND ALETA ARE HELPLESS PRISONERS IN THE GARDEN. FOR THE GARDEN WAS DESIGNED SO THE QUEEN WOULD HAVE PRIVACY. THE WALLS ARE HIGH, NO WINDOWS OVERLOOK IT, AND THE TALL TREES DROWN THEIR CALLS FOR HELP.

ARN REPORTS THE WORDS HE OVERHEARD MODRED SAY TO HIS HALF-BROTHERS. "I CANNOT SEE WHAT THAT HAS TO DO WITH YOUR MOTHER'S ABSENCE," SAYS VAL, "BUT IT IS WELL TO INVESTIGATE ANY OF MODRED'S SLY SCHEMES."

AT THE GATE TO THE QUEEN'S GARDEN STANDS A PUZZLED GUARD. "I CANNOT LET YOU INTO THE GARDEN, SIR VALIANT. THE DOOR IS LOCKED AND THE KEY REMOVED."

9-29-63   1390

"COME, ARN, WE WILL GET A LADDER. EVEN IF WE DO NOT FIND YOUR MOTHER WE WILL DO A GOOD DEED IF WE DISCOVER WHAT MODRED IS UP TO."

NEXT WEEK – *A Chilly Picnic*

HAL FOSTER

Prince Valiant
IN THE DAYS OF KING ARTHUR
WRITTEN AND ILLUSTRATED BY HAROLD R FOSTER

Our Story: ALETA MISLAYS THE TWINS AND BEGINS A SEARCH. THE TWINS TURN UP, BUT NOW ALETA IS MISSING. PRINCE VALIANT BORROWS A LADDER, FOR THE ONLY PLACE HE HAS NOT SEARCHED IS THE QUEEN'S PRIVATE GARDEN, AND THE DOOR IS LOCKED AND THE KEY MISSING.

SIR LAUNCELOT IS PACING UP AND DOWN IN THE MOONLIGHT, TRYING TO KEEP WARM, AND ALETA, WRAPPED IN HIS GREAT CLOAK, IS HUDDLED ON THE PAVILION STEPS. *"RATHER CHILLY FOR A PICNIC, ISN'T IT?"* ASKS VAL.

"HAVE KAREN AND VALETA BEEN FOUND?" ARE ALETA'S FIRST WORDS. *"MY SWORD WILL HAVE A PICNIC WHEN I FIND WHOEVER LOCKED US IN HERE!"* BELLOWS LAUNCELOT.

ARN IS SENT SCURRYING TO FETCH CLOAKS AND BLANKETS WHILE VAL FILLS A HAMPER IN THE PANTRY. THEN THEY LOWER THE LADDER INTO THE GARDEN.

"OURS WILL BE A VERY FROSTY PICNIC," SAYS VAL, *"BUT IT IS PAST MIDNIGHT, AND IF I GUESS RIGHT, WITH THE DAWN THE PRANKSTERS WILL SOMEHOW FIND THE KEY. THEY WILL FIND YOU TWO, AND WE WILL DISCOVER WHO THEY ARE."*

WITH CATLIKE TREAD SIR MODRED REPLACES THE KEY AND SILENTLY UNLOCKS THE GARDEN DOOR......

..... WHILE SOME OF HIS FOLLOWERS MAKE A GREAT TO-DO PRETENDING TO SEARCH FOR ALETA, THEREBY AWAKENING EVERYONE.

1391   10-6-63

WHEN SUFFICIENT WITNESSES HAVE GATHERED, MODRED EXCLAIMS: *"THAT DOOR, WHERE DOES IT LEAD? TO THE QUEEN'S GARDEN? THAT IS THE ONLY PLACE WE HAVE NOT SEARCHED. OPEN IT!"*

NEXT WEEK— **The Shadow of Death**

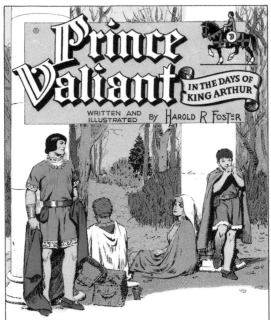

Prince Valiant
IN THE DAYS OF KING ARTHUR
WRITTEN AND ILLUSTRATED BY HAROLD R FOSTER

Our Story : WITH THE DAWN COMES THE SQUEAK OF HINGES AS THE GARDEN GATE IS OPENED. AT LAST THEY WILL FIND OUT WHY, AND BY WHOM, LAUNCELOT AND ALETA HAD BEEN LOCKED IN.

MODRED COMES DOWN THE PATH FOLLOWED BY A NUMBER OF HIS FRIENDS. HE STOPS IN MOCK SURPRISE. *"WE HAVE BEEN SEARCHING FOR THE LADY ALETA, BELIEVING HER LOST."*

"OUR HUMBLE PARDON, FOR I SEE WE INTRUDE ON A TRYST." THEN THE LOOK OF TRIUMPH FADES AND HIS FACE GOES WHITE..... PRINCE VALIANT AND ARN STEP FROM BEHIND THE PILLARS.

HIS SORRY PLOT TO CREATE A SCANDAL AND SOW THE SEEDS OF JEALOUSY AND ANGER HAVE GONE ASTRAY IN THE FACE OF THIS RESPECTABLE FAMILY PICNIC. SOMEONE IN THE GROUP BEHIND HIM LAUGHS.

"SIR MODRED, YOUR WORDS REFLECT ON MY WIFE'S GOOD NAME!" THE COLD MENACE IN THESE FEW WORDS CAN MEAN ONLY ONE THING: A DUEL, AND MODRED'S CERTAIN DEATH. HE IS NO COWARD, BUT HE MUST LIVE TO FULFILL HIS AMBITIONS.

SO HE STIFLES HIS FIERCE PRIDE AND APOLOGIZES MOST HUMBLY. HIS FRIENDS AND FOLLOWERS STAND IN MINGLED SURPRISE AND CONTEMPT.

SOONER OR LATER THE FULL EXTENT OF HIS PLOT WILL BE FOUND OUT AND A FIGHT WITH PRINCE VALIANT INEVITABLE. HE PACKS HIS BAGS.

1392   10-13-63

AND MODRED RIDES TO HIS HOME IN LOTHIAN, THERE TO SCHEME AND PLOT TO WREST THE CROWN FROM KING ARTHUR.

NEXT WEEK— *Saxons in the Vale!*

Prince Valiant
IN THE DAYS OF KING ARTHUR

WRITTEN AND ILLUSTRATED BY HAROLD R. FOSTER

Our Story: SIR MODRED'S PLOT WENT ASTRAY; INSTEAD OF TRAGEDY IT BROUGHT ONLY LAUGHTER. HE DEEMS IT PRUDENT TO LEAVE CAMELOT FOR A WHILE. RIDING NORTH HE AND HIS RETAINERS REACH THE WHITE HORSE VALE AND SEE A SAXON WAR BAND ENCAMPED.

A RIDER IS SENT BACK TO CAMELOT WITH THE NEWS.

"IT MUST BE A SCOUTING PARTY," MUSES THE KING, "FOR NO ARMY COULD MOVE IN THE WINTER, WITH FOOD SCARCE AND RIVERS IN FLOOD. IT WOULD BE USELESS TO SEND CAVALRY AGAINST THEM; THERE IS NOT ENOUGH FORAGE FOR THE HORSES."

"WE WILL SEND A SCOUTING PARTY TO OBSERVE THEM AND FIND OUT WHAT THEY ARE UP TO. SELECT THREE YOUNG KNIGHTS WHO WISH TO DISTINGUISH THEMSELVES, AND THREE LADS TO ACT AS MESSENGERS."

HOW OFTEN HAS ALETA PACKED HER HUSBAND'S SADDLEBAGS WHEN HE WENT OFF TO FACE SOME HARDY FOE. NOW IT IS HER SON'S BAG SHE PACKS.

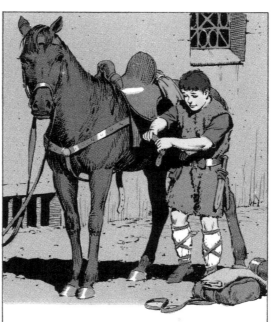

FOR ARN HAS BEEN CHOSEN AS ONE OF THE MESSENGERS, BECAUSE OF HIS FINE ACTIONS DURING THE NORTH WALES CAMPAIGN.

1393   10-20

VAL WOULD LIKE TO GO ON THIS EXPEDITION, BUT HE HAS SERIOUS WORK TO DO, PLANNING THE WAR GAMES THAT ARE TO PREPARE THE KNIGHTS FOR THE SUMMER CAMPAIGNS.

NEXT WEEK — **The War Band**

HAL FOSTER

Our Story: WINTER IS ON THE WANE. STEADY RAINS MAKE THE GROUND SOFT AND EACH BROOK A TORRENT. THE SCOUTING PARTY IS THOROUGHLY MISERABLE, ALL EXCEPT PRINCE ARN, WHO IS IMPATIENT FOR ADVENTURES TO BEGIN.

AT LAST THE LITTLE GROUP OF SCOUTS ARRIVES AT WHITE HORSE VALE, WHERE THE SAXON WAR BAND WAS LAST SEEN, BUT THE VALE IS EMPTY.

ARN VOLUNTEERS TO INVESTIGATE WHILE THE OTHERS KEEP WATCH. THE COOKING FIRES ARE COLD, THE SOFT GROUND SHOWS MANY FOOT-PRINTS, BUT AT LAST HE FINDS WHERE ALL THE PRINTS POINT IN ONE DIRECTION.

BY FOLLOWING THE DIRECTION OF THE FOOTPRINTS THEY COME AT LAST UPON THE SAXON CAMP.

THE THREE YOUNG KNIGHTS RECORD THEIR NUMBER, EQUIPMENT AND APPARENT ERRAND, AND ONE OF THE MESSENGERS IS SENT BACK TO CAMELOT WITH THE INFORMATION.

"THEY CARRY NO BANNERS, SO THEY ARE SCOUTING, AND THEY HAVE FOUND THE EASY ROUTE INTO THE HEART OF BRITAIN. NOW WE MUST FIND OUT WHETHER THEY ARE HENGIST'S MEN FROM KENT OR BETHWALD'S MEN FROM ESSEX."

"SIRS, OWEN AND I ARE SMALL. WE CAN CREEP THROUGH THE HEATHER AND GET CLOSE ENOUGH TO MAKE OUT THE INSIGNIA OF THEIR CHIEF."

1394   10-27-63

THE BOYS RIDE SWIFTLY AHEAD FOR WHAT THEY THINK WILL BE A DAY'S MARCH. THERE THEY TETHER THEIR HORSES AND AWAIT THE COMING OF THE SAXONS.

NEXT WEEK— **Capture**

Prince Valiant

IN THE DAYS OF KING ARTHUR

WRITTEN AND ILLUSTRATED BY HAROLD R FOSTER

Our Story: PRINCE ARN AND OWEN CONCEAL THEMSELVES AMID THE HEATHER ON THE HILLSIDE ABOVE THE PLACE WHERE THE SAXON WAR BAND IS EXPECTED TO CAMP. THEIR MISSION: TO FIND OUT WHETHER THEY ARE OF THE WEST SAXONS OR THE EAST SAXONS.

"LOOK, SEVERAL OF THEM ARE COMING OUR WAY," EXCLAIMS OWEN, "TO GATHER FIREWOOD, I GUESS."
"NO, THEY ARE FULLY ARMED," WHISPERS ARN, "THEY MUST BE SENTRIES. IF THEY TAKE THEIR PLACES ABOVE US, WE WILL BE SURROUNDED."

"WE CAN CREEP UP THROUGH THE HEATHER AND GET BEHIND THAT SENTRY, THEN MY VIRGIN SWORD CAN BE BLOODIED AND I BECOME A MAN!" BUT ARN REFUSES, "WE HAVE A MISSION TO COMPLETE FIRST."

ARN IS LEADING THE WAY TOWARD THE CAMP WHEN A SHOUT OF WARNING, FOLLOWED BY A SCREAM OF PAIN, MAKES HIM TURN. OWEN HAS TURNED BACK TO WIN PERSONAL GLORY. "THE HOT-HEADED FOOL!" EXCLAIMS ARN, "HE HAS BETRAYED US!"

OWEN REALIZES TOO LATE THAT HIS ONLY AVENUE OF ESCAPE IS THE HORSES, AND HE MUST TAKE BOTH TO AVOID PURSUIT. SEEING TWO HORSES, THE SAXONS WILL KNOW THAT THERE IS ONE MORE SPY NEAR BY.

ARN HAS A FEW MINUTES TO MAKE PLANS BEFORE THE SEARCH STARTS. HE MUST SURELY BE DISCOVERED, AND THE SAXONS DO NOT TAKE PRISONERS.

SPEAR POINTS ARE PRODDING THE HEATHER, NEARER AND NEARER THEY COME.

11-3-63   1395

HAL FOSTER

PRINCE ARN STANDS ERECT AND WALKS BOLDLY TOWARD THE ENEMY CAMP.

NEXT WEEK— **Boltarson**

Prince Valiant
IN THE DAYS OF KING ARTHUR
WRITTEN AND ILLUSTRATED By HAROLD R. FOSTER

Our Story: PRINCE ARN STANDS UP BOLDLY BEFORE THE SEARCHERS REACH HIM. "MAY THE GODDESS OF LUCK GRANT ME A GLIB TONGUE, THAT I MAY LIE CONVINCINGLY," HE PRAYS. THEN HE WALKS CALMLY TOWARD THE SAXON CAMP.

"TAKE ME TO YOUR CHIEFTAIN," HE COMMANDS. "IT WILL BE LESS WORK IF WE TAKE ONLY YOUR HEAD," ANSWERS A BARBARIAN, DRAWING HIS SWORD. "HARM ME AND YOU ANSWER TO MY FATHER, BOLTAR, THE SEA KING!"

ARN IS TAKEN TO THEIR CHIEFTAIN, FOR, EVEN AMONG THE SAXONS THE NAME OF BOLTAR IS KNOWN, AND THE DEEDS OF THE VIKING WITH THE FLAMING BEARD ARE TOLD IN SONG AND STORY..... AND PRINCE ARN'S HAIR IS RED. "I HAVE HEARD IT TOLD THAT BOLTAR HAS A SON," REMARKS THE CHIEF. "SO YOU ARE BOLTARSON. WHY ARE YOU HERE?"

"I WAS SENT TO CAMELOT AS HOSTAGE AND TO LEARN THE WAYS OF THE BRITONS. IT IS NOT FOR ME. I CHOSE THIS WAY TO ESCAPE, THE SOONER TO JOIN MY FATHER'S SHIP AND LEARN THE WAYS OF FIGHTING MEN."

OWEN IS NOW A WARRIOR, FOR HE HAS KILLED AN ENEMY AND ESCAPED, BUT IN DOING SO HE ABANDONED HIS FRIEND ARN AND HIS MISSION.

HE REPORTS ARN CAPTURED BY THE SAXONS AND PRESUMED DEAD. HE DOES NOT TELL OF THE HOT-HEADED DEED THAT DEFEATED THE MISSION.

AS THE ONLY MESSENGER LEFT, OWEN IS SENT TO CAMELOT WITH THE LATEST REPORTS. HE ALSO MUST FACE ARN'S PARENTS, AND REPROACHES HIMSELF BITTERLY FOR HIS WILLFULNESS.

NEXT WEEK - **A Painful Duty**

11-10   1396

Prince Valiant
IN THE DAYS OF KING ARTHUR
WRITTEN AND ILLUSTRATED BY Harold R Foster

Our Story: THE THREE YOUNG KNIGHTS WHO ARE SCOUTING THE WAR BAND SEND OWEN BACK TO CAMELOT WITH THEIR REPORT AND TO TELL OF PRINCE ARN'S CAPTURE.

A FEW DAYS LATER HE STANDS BEFORE THE KING AND GIVES HIS MESSAGE, BUT WHEN IT COMES TIME TO TELL OF ARN'S CAPTURE, HE STAMMERS AND HANGS HIS HEAD.

FOR AT CAMELOT THE YOUNG PAGE AND SQUIRE IS SO THOROUGHLY TRAINED IN THE KNIGHTLY TRADITION THAT TO BE ANYTHING LESS IS TO FEEL SHAME.

BUT WHEN HE FACES ARN'S PARENTS HE CANNOT LONGER HIDE THE TRUTH. WITH TEARS STREAKING HIS TRAVEL-STAINED CHEEKS HE BLURTS OUT THE WHOLE STORY. OF HOW HE SOUGHT SELF-GLORY, HAD KILLED AN ENEMY TO GAIN WARRIOR'S STATUS, BUT IN ESCAPING HAD TAKEN BOTH HORSES AND ABANDONED ARN TO HIS FATE.

"DON'T LOOK SO TRAGIC, OWEN. ARN HAS BEEN IN TIGHT PLACES BEFORE, HAS HE NOT, ALETA? WITH HIS READY WIT AND COOL HEAD HE HAS MOST LIKELY FINISHED HIS MISSION AND IS ON HIS WAY BACK. I MAY EVEN RIDE OUT TO MEET HIM ON THE MORROW!"

SO OFTEN DOES EACH ASSURE THE OTHER THAT ARN IS SAFE, THAT THEY BEGIN TO BELIEVE IT.... ALMOST. AND THE MOTHER DREAMS OF A WARM AND HELPLESS BABY AND A CHILD WHO RAN TO HER FOR LOVE AND COMFORT. WHILE THE FATHER REMEMBERS THE STURDY LAD, HALF MAN, HALF BOY, THE FLEDGLING EAGLE.

HAL FOSTER

NEXT WEEK— **The Captive**

1397

11-17

Prince Valiant
IN THE DAYS OF KING ARTHUR
WRITTEN AND ILLUSTRATED BY Harold R Foster

Our Story: PRINCE VALIANT LEAVES CAMELOT IN SEARCH OF HIS SON, PRINCE ARN, REPORTED A CAPTIVE OF A SAXON WAR PARTY. HE HOLDS ARVAK TO A LEISURELY WALK SO ALETA WILL SEE THAT HE IS NOT AT ALL ANXIOUS.

BUT ONCE OUT OF SIGHT SETS A FURIOUS PACE, FOR WELL HE KNOWS THE SAXON WAY WITH PRISONERS.

OWEN GUIDES HIM TO WHERE THE THREE YOUNG KNIGHTS ARE KEEPING WATCH ON THE SAXONS. FROM THE EDGE OF THE DOWNS THEY LOOK DOWN INTO THE VALE.......

.....AND THERE IS ARN IN ANIMATED CONVERSATION WITH THE CHIEFTAIN AND, AS THEY PUSH ON TO THE WEST, HE SEEMS TO BE POINTING OUT THE WAY.
A TERRIBLE THOUGHT COMES TO VAL. HAS ARN BEEN PUT TO TORTURE TO MAKE HIM ACT AS A GUIDE?

AS ARN WALKED INTO THEIR CAMP OF HIS OWN FREE WILL, CLAIMING TO BE THE SON OF BOLTAR THE VIKING SEA KING, AND SPEAKING THE NORTHMAN'S TONGUE, HE HAS NOT BEEN HARMED, THOUGH UNDER CONSTANT GUARD. HE KNOWS THE COUNTRY WELL, HAVING PASSED THIS WAY ON THE NORTH WALES CAMPAIGN.

"WHAT LIES AHEAD, BOLTARSON?" ASKS THE CHIEFTAIN. "PERIL," ANSWERS ARN. "TO THE NORTH A LAND LAID WASTE AND BARREN OF FOOD. TO THE SOUTH, THE HEARTLAND OF BRITAIN, BUT PROTECTED BY THE WANSDYKE."

ARN GUIDES THEM TO THE WANSDYKE. "KING VORTIGERN BUILT THIS TO HOLD BACK THE FIERCE TRIBES OF THE NORTH. IT HAS NOT BEEN USED SINCE KING ARTHUR BROUGHT THEM UNDER HIS RULE."

1398

HAL FOSTER

COULD IT BE POSSIBLE THAT PRINCE ARN, SON OF SIR VALIANT, IS A TRAITOR, WILLINGLY SHOWING THEIR ENEMIES THE BEST WAY TO ATTACK CAMELOT?

NEXT WEEK—**Arn's Price**

11-24

Prince Valiant
IN THE DAYS OF KING ARTHUR

WRITTEN AND ILLUSTRATED

BY HAROLD R. FOSTER

Our Story: THE SAXON CHIEFTAIN INTENDS TO KILL HIS PRISONER WHEN HE HAS GOTTEN ALL THE INFORMATION ARN POSSESSES. "HOW BEST CAN WE PASS THE WANSDYKE?" HE ASKS.

"YOU NEED NOT PASS IT," ANSWERS ARN. "THE BEST WAY INTO THE HEARTLAND OF BRITAIN IS UP THE THAMES VALLEY, THEN TURN SOUTHWARD BEFORE ENCOUNTERING THE DYKE. ONLY ONE STRONG POINT WILL YOU PASS, A FORT ON BADON HILL, BUT IT HAS LONG SINCE FALLEN INTO RUIN."

"WHY DOES THE SON OF BOLTAR, A VIKING, GIVE ALL THIS INFORMATION TO A SAXON?" THE CHIEFTAIN DEMANDS. BEFORE ANSWERING, ARN MAKES A SILENT PRAYER (MAY THE SHADE OF ANANIAS GUIDE MY TONGUE THAT I MAY LIE CONVINCINGLY!)

"AS A HOSTAGE IN CAMELOT I STUDIED ITS WEAK POINTS, FOR MY FATHER BOLTAR LONGS FOR ITS RICHES. BUT BOLTAR, INVINCIBLE AT SEA, HAS NOT THE SKILL FOR A LAND SIEGE. I GIVE YOU THIS INFORMATION FOR A SHARE IN THE PLUNDER AND SAFE RETURN TO MY FATHER'S SHIP."

PRINCE VALIANT WATCHES AS THE SAXONS' SCOUTING PARTY TURNS BACK, UNAWARE THAT HIS COMPANIONS LOOK AT HIM WITH PITY. FOR IT SEEMS CLEAR TO THEM THAT HIS SON HAS TURNED TRAITOR TO SAVE HIS OWN SKIN. WHAT A DISGRACE!

THEY ARE RIGHT IN A WAY. ARN IS PLANNING TO SAVE HIS SKIN.

NEXT WEEK— **The Hunt**

1399

12-1

Prince Valiant
IN THE DAYS OF KING ARTHUR
WRITTEN AND ILLUSTRATED BY HAROLD R FOSTER

Our Story: THE LEADER OF THE SAXON SCOUTING PARTY FINDS ARN'S KNOWLEDGE OF THE COUNTRY USEFUL. "OUR FOOD SUPPLY IS RUNNING LOW. IS THERE ANY VILLAGE NEARBY WE CAN RAID?" ASKS THE CHIEFTAIN.

"RUMORS OF A SAXON RAID WOULD SURELY REACH KING ARTHUR, AND HE WOULD BE ALERT TO GUARD AGAINST A SURPRISE ATTACK FROM THIS DIRECTION," ANSWERS ARN. "BUT CALL UP YOUR BEST HUNTERS, AND I WILL LEAD THEM TO A HERD OF DEER."

ARN LEADS THE WAY TO THE TOP OF THE DOWNS, KNOWING THAT EVERY MOVE IS BEING WATCHED BY THE THREE KNIGHTS SENT TO SPY ON THE SAXONS.

"IF THE HUNTERS WILL TAKE THEIR STAND ON EITHER SIDE OF THAT DRAW, WE THREE WILL CIRCLE THE COPSE AND DRIVE THE DEER THIS WAY."

ARN AND HIS EVER-PRESENT GUARDS ARE JUST READY TO BEGIN THEIR DRIVE WHEN A MOUNTED KNIGHT IS SEEN AGAINST THE SKYLINE. THERE IS NO MISTAKING THAT RED STALLION; PRINCE VALIANT HAS COME TO RESCUE HIS SON. "RUN! RUN FOR THE WOODS!" SCREAMS ARN.

URGED ON BY THE THUNDERING HOOFBEATS THEY SPEED FOR THE SAFETY OF THE TANGLED WOOD. THEN ARN TRIPS IN THE HEATHER AND GOES DOWN.

THE GUARDS WILL PAY WITH THEIR LIVES IF BOLTARSON ESCAPES. IT WOULD BE DEATH ALSO TO FACE AN ARMED AND MOUNTED KNIGHT. THEY WATCH THE KNIGHT SEARCH THE HEATHER.

THEY ARE TOO FAR AWAY TO HEAR ARN WHISPER: "DO NOT NOTICE ME, FATHER, FOR I MUST RETURN TO THE SAXONS. SOON I WILL KNOW THEIR BATTLE PLANS...." THEN HE EXPLAINS HIS FUTURE SCHEME.

NEXT WEEK—The Digging of Arn's Grave

12-8-63   1400

Prince Valiant
IN THE DAYS OF KING ARTHUR
WRITTEN AND ILLUSTRATED BY HAROLD R FOSTER

Our Story: PRINCE VALIANT RIDES TO RESCUE HIS SON FROM THE SAXONS, BUT ARN REFUSES TO BE RESCUED. "I KNOW TOO MUCH OF THEIR WAR PLANS FOR THE SUMMER CAMPAIGN. IF I ESCAPE, THESE PLANS WILL BE CHANGED."

ARN WHISPERS HIS PLAN FOR A FUTURE RESCUE. THEN VAL PRETENDS TO SCAN THE HEATHER. FINALLY GIVING UP, HE RIDES AWAY TO THE SOUTH AND ARN CREEPS BACK TO HIS GUARDS.

THE HUNT IS COMPLETED AND ENOUGH VENISON BROUGHT BACK TO RELIEVE THE HUNGER OF THE SAXON SCOUTING BAND.

THIS IS THE SECOND TIME BOLTARSON (ARN) HAS RETURNED OF HIS OWN FREE WILL. THAT HIS BOW AND SWORD ARE RETURNED SHOWS HE IS NO LONGER UNDER SUSPICION. HOWEVER, HIS TWO GUARDS STILL FOLLOW HIS EVERY MOVE.

UNDER THE SHADOW OF BADON HILL ARN GIVES THE SAXON CHIEFTAIN HIS MOST IMPORTANT INFORMATION. "AN OLD ROMAN ROAD CROSSES THE WHITE HORSE VALE AND REACHES THE CREST OF THE DOWNS BY WAY OF YONDER SIDE VALLEY. BEYOND, THE FERTILE HEART OF BRITAIN AND ALL ITS RICHES AWAITS A CONQUEROR."

"IT IS NECESSARY THAT OUR SCOUTING BAND REMAIN UNDISCOVERED. IF IT BE YOUR WISH I WILL SCOUT THE VALLEY. SHOULD WE MEET ANYONE, I SPEAK THEIR TONGUE, AND THESE TWO CAN DRESS LIKE PEASANTS."

"I HOPE MY FATHER REMEMBERS THE PLAN," PRAYS ARN. "HERE HE COMES RIGHT ON TIME!" "OH! WHAT A SON." MURMURS VAL.

12-15-63

HAL FOSTER

BUT WHAT DOES THIS MEAN? THE YOUNG KNIGHTS THE KING HAD SENT TO SPY ON THE SAXONS ARE DIGGING A GRAVE FOR ARN!

NEXT WEEK — **The Untouched Grave**

1401

Prince Valiant
IN THE DAYS OF KING ARTHUR
WRITTEN AND ILLUSTRATED BY Harold R Foster

Our Story: PRINCE ARN LEADS THE WAY UP THE VALLEY BY WHICH THE SAXON ARMY MIGHT CONQUER BRITAIN. ALTHOUGH ARN DOES NOT REALIZE IT, THE FATE OF THE KINGDOM WILL BE DECIDED IN THE NEXT FEW MINUTES.

"HAVE FUN, SIRE!" CALLS ARN AS HE STEPS ASIDE TO LET ARVAK THUNDER BY. TWICE THE 'SINGING SWORD' GLEAMS IN THE SUNLIGHT, THEN PRINCE VALIANT RIDES BACK.

ARN HAS SLIT A WIDE GASH IN HIS JERKIN AND IS STAINING IT IN BLOOD. *"THIS IS THE FIRST FAVOR A SAXON HAS EVER DONE FOR ME,"* HE ANNOUNCES.

WHEN TWO DAYS GO BY AND BOLTARSON HAS NOT RETURNED, THE CHIEFTAIN CALLS ON HIS BEST TRACKER AND THEY GO IN SEARCH.

"EACH ONE CLEFT WITH ONE MIGHTY STROKE, AND BY A KNIGHT, FOR SEE, HIS HORSE IS SHOD," EXPLAINS THE TRACKER. *"THE BOY WAS KILLED, TOO, FOR HERE IS HIS BLOODIED GARMENT ALSO SLIT BY A SWORD STROKE!"*

AND THERE IS ALSO A FRESHLY TURNED GRAVE. *"SHALL WE DIG HIM UP TO MAKE SURE?" "NO,"* ANSWERS THE CHIEFTAIN, *"HE WAS A BRAVE LAD, LET HIM REST. WHOEVER KILLED HIM MUST HAVE THOUGHT HIM NOBLE ENOUGH TO GIVE HIM BURIAL."*

THE WATCHERS ON THE HILLTOP SEE THE SAXONS TURN BACK. THEN AND ONLY THEN FATHER AND SON GREET EACH OTHER WHOLEHEARTEDLY.

NOW THEY MUST HURRY BACK TO CAMELOT TO INFORM KING ARTHUR. FROM WHAT ARN HAS LEARNED, THE SAXONS ARE PREPARING FOR ONE GREAT CAMPAIGN TO CONQUER ALL BRITAIN.

NEXT WEEK – **"So I Died"**

1402   12-22-63

Our Story: PRINCE VALIANT SETS A PACE THAT TAXES THE ENDURANCE OF HORSE AND MAN. THE SCOUTS HE LEADS ARE ANXIOUS FOR THE COMFORTS OF CAMELOT, FOR THEY HAVE SPENT THREE WEEKS IN FROST AND RAIN WITH NO OTHER COVER THAN THEIR CLOAKS, UNABLE TO BUILD EVEN THE FLIMSIEST SHELTER FOR FEAR OF BETRAYING THEIR PRESENCE TO THE SAXONS.

VAL LOSES NO TIME IN PRESENTING HIMSELF TO THE KING. FOR SPRING HAS COME AND SOON ARMIES CAN BE ON THE MARCH.

THE THREE BEDRAGGLED SCOUTS REPORT ON ALL THEY HAVE SEEN. FOR SOME TIME THE KING IS SILENT, THINKING. AT LAST HE SAYS: "IT IS NOT OFTEN WE INVITE A BOY TO OUR COUNCIL CHAMBER, BUT YOUR VENTURE-SOME SON SEEMS TO HAVE HAD THE MORE INTIMATE CONTACT WITH THE SAXONS. SUMMON HIM, SIR VALIANT!"

"NOW, PRINCE ARN, WHY DID YOU SHOW THE SAXON SCOUTS THE ROUTE BY WHICH THEY COULD ATTACK CAMELOT?"
"SIRE, I WAS MOST USEFUL TO OUR ENEMIES," GRINS ARN, "BUT I SHOWED THEM ONLY WHAT THEY WOULD HAVE FOUND OUT FOR THEM-SELVES. AND I EARNED THEIR CONFIDENCE."
"AND WHY DID YOU REFUSE SIR VALIANT'S RESCUE?"

"I KNEW THE INVASION ROUTE. HAD I ESCAPED WITH THAT KNOWLEDGE THE ROUTE MIGHT HAVE BEEN CHANGED, SO I PLANNED MY BURIAL, TAKING MY KNOWLEDGE TO THE GRAVE," ANSWERS ARN IN MOCK GRIEF.

NOW THEY ARE FREE FOR A REUNION, BUT IT IS ARN WHO CANNOT CONTROL HIS IMPATIENCE

ALETA HAS HER MOMENT, BUT THERE IS A GRAIN OF SADNESS; FOR NOW SHE HAS TWO TO WELCOME HOME.... AND TWO TO BID FAREWELL.

NEXT WEEK - **The New Man**

1403   12-29-63

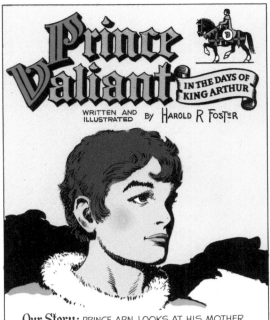

Prince Valiant
IN THE DAYS OF KING ARTHUR
WRITTEN AND ILLUSTRATED BY HAROLD R FOSTER

Our Story: PRINCE ARN LOOKS AT HIS MOTHER AS IF SEEING HER FOR THE FIRST TIME. TILL NOW HE HAS ALWAYS LOOKED TO HER FOR INSTRUCTIONS, ADVICE, EVEN PROTECTION. SHE HAS CHANGED SOMEHOW, AS IF IT IS SHE WHO NEEDS PROTECTION.

AS THEY WALK TOWARD THE PALACE HE OFFERS HIS ARM TO HELP HER OVER THE ROUGH COBBLES.

HE STANDS BESIDE HER PROUDLY, NOTING HER POISE AND READY WIT. ALETA SMILES. SHE HAS NOT CHANGED A BIT. IT IS HER SON WHO HAS CHANGED. HE HAS GROWN UP. THE FLEDGLING NOW HAS WINGS.

ARN JOINS HIS FATHER IN THE ARMORY, WHERE THERE IS GREAT ACTIVITY. FOR PREPARATIONS ARE GOING FORWARD FOR THE GREAT SPRING TOURNAMENT THAT IS THE FINAL TRAINING FOR THE SUMMER CAMPAIGNS.

GUESTS ARRIVE DAILY, NONE MORE DISTINGUISHED THAN COUNT BRECEY OF BRITTANY, MASTER OF WIDE LANDS AND MANY CASTLES.

HE HESITATES BESIDE A LAUGHING GROUP, HIS ATTENTION CAUGHT BY A FACE WITH EYES THAT TWINKLE WITH MERRIMENT—ALETA'S.

1404

1-5-64

"THAT WOMAN, THE ONE WITH GOLDEN HAIR AND GREY EYES. FIND OUT WHAT YOU CAN ABOUT HER," HE ORDERS A RETAINER.

THAT A HANDSOME, DARK-EYED STRANGER HAS FOLLOWED HER ALL DAY, STARING, BOTHERS ALETA NOT AT ALL. EVER SINCE SHE CAN REMEMBER, MEN HAVE ADMIRED HER, IT IS NOT EVEN WORTH MENTIONING. NEXT WEEK— The Manslayer

Our Story: THE POWERFUL COUNT BRECEY OF BRITTANY, HANDSOME AND RUTHLESS, HAS NEVER BEEN DENIED ANYTHING HE WANTS. NOW HIS SOMBRE EYES FOLLOW QUEEN ALETA WHEREVER SHE GOES.

A RETAINER REPORTS: "SHE IS QUEEN ALETA AND WIFE OF SIR VALIANT, A PRINCE OF SOME OBSCURE LAND TO THE NORTH, AND SHE HAS FOUR CHILDREN."

"IN THAT CASE I SHALL MAKE HER MY WIFE AS SOON AS SHE IS WIDOWED. HER CHILDREN MAY SOME DAY BE KINGS OR QUEENS. AS THEIR STEPFATHER MY POWER WILL BE GREAT."

HE SENDS FOR HIS COUSIN, HUGO, HIS CHAMPION AND AN ACCOMPLISHED KILLER OF MEN. "YOU HAVE ALWAYS WANTED THE FIEF AND CASTLE OF GLANDON. KILL ME THIS SIR VALIANT DURING THE TOURNAMENT AND IT IS YOURS."

HUGO GOES INTO THE PRACTICE YARD WHERE KNIGHTS ARE TRAINING FOR THE TOURNAMENT. THERE ARE PRIZES, GLORY AND APPLAUSE TO BE WON AT THE WAR GAMES, BUT WORD HAS GONE AROUND THAT THERE WILL BE A LIFE-AND-DEATH STRUGGLE WITH THE SAXONS THIS YEAR, AND THEY TRAIN IN EARNEST.

HE WATCHES PRINCE VALIANT INTENTLY. "HE IS SKILLFUL AND MUCH MORE AGILE THAN I, BUT MY GREATER STRENGTH WILL PREVAIL, AND HE HOLDS HIS SHIELD TOO LOW. HIS ONLY ADVANTAGE IS IN THAT GREAT WAR HORSE. I MUST CONTRIVE TO WOUND IT"!

THEN BRECEY, OVERCONFIDENT OF HIS POWER, MAKES A MISTAKE. "SUMMON MISTRESS ALETA. I WISH TO CONVERSE WITH HER."

1405   1-12

"SIRE, HER ANSWER IS, 'TELL YOUR MASTER THAT I, ALETA, QUEEN OF THE MISTY ISLES, WILL GRANT HIM AUDIENCE IF HE BE PROPERLY PRESENTED.'"

NEXT WEEK—*A Strand of Wire*

Our Story: IN BRITTANY COUNT BRECEY HAS THE POWER OF LIFE AND DEATH OVER HIS SUBJECTS AND TAKES WHAT HE WANTS. HERE AT CAMELOT THINGS ARE DIFFERENT, AND THE WOMAN HE HAS CHOSEN TO BE HIS WIFE HAS GIVEN HIM A SHARP REBUFF.

THAT SHE IS MARRIED AND HAS FOUR CHILDREN MAKES NO DIFFERENCE TO HIM, FOR HE HAS PLANNED TO MAKE HER A WIDOW.
SO BRECEY HUMBLES HIMSELF AND MAKES AN APOLOGY. AND WHY NOT? HE CAN MAKE HER PAY FOR IT AFTER SHE BECOMES HIS WIFE.

"PARDON ME, FAIR LADY, IF MY MANNERS SEEM BRUSQUE, FOR I AM A LONELY MAN. WEALTH, MANY CASTLES AND WIDE SUNNY LANDS ARE MINE, BUT I HAVE NEVER KNOWN THE SOFTENING INFLUENCE OF A GOOD WOMAN."

HUGO MAKES HIS REPORT: "SIR VALIANT IS A GOOD FIGHTER. I CAN KILL HIM FOR YOU EASILY IF WE FIGHT AFOOT, BUT MOUNTED ON THAT HUGE, WELL-TRAINED STALLION, IT IS ANOTHER MATTER. WE MUST CRIPPLE THE RED STALLION."

IT IS THE DAY BEFORE THE GREAT TOURNAMENT AND A BALL IS HELD. BRECEY IS EVER AT ALETA'S SIDE, FOR, TO HIS WAY OF THINKING, SHE IS ALREADY HIS.
"I HAD PLANNED TO LAY THE CROWN OF VICTORY AT YOUR FEET AS QUEEN OF BEAUTY, BUT," HE SIGHS, "I WOUNDED MY SWORD HAND IN PRACTICE."

1-19-64

1406

"NOW, HUGO, ERE THE DAWN, YOU MUST FIND SIR VALIANT'S WAR HORSE AND WIND THIS WIRE TIGHTLY ABOUT ITS PASTERN BELOW THE FETLOCK. SEE THAT THE HAIR HIDES IT. THEN YOU WILL BE ASSURED OF VICTORY."

NEXT WEEK— **Hugo Meets Arvak**

Prince Valiant
IN THE DAYS OF KING ARTHUR
WRITTEN AND ILLUSTRATED BY Harold R Foster

Our Story: IN THE DARKNESS JUST BEFORE DAWN OF THE DAY OF THE GREAT TOURNAMENT HUGO GOES TO THE PICKET LINE WHERE THE KNIGHTS' MOUNTS ARE UNDER GUARD.

ON THE PRETENSE OF CARING FOR HIS OWN STEED HUGO SEEKS OUT ARVAK, PRINCE VALIANT'S GREAT WAR HORSE.

AND NOW THIS WIRE, WOUND TIGHTLY AROUND THE PASTERN AND HIDDEN BY THE HAIR OF THE FETLOCK, WILL NUMB THE FOOT, AND SIR VALIANT WILL CONTEND IN THE LISTS ON A LAME HORSE.

HUGO, WITH A CRACKED RIB, HAS JUST LEARNED WHAT EVERY-ONE IN CAMELOT KNOWS: THAT NO ONE TAKES LIBERTIES WITH THE GREAT RED STALLION. IN A BLIND RAGE HE DRAWS HIS SAX KNIFE TO HAMSTRING THE HATED HORSE.

ARVAK SENSES THAT THIS IS AN ENEMY AND IS FIRST TO ATTACK, BUT HUGO SAVES HIMSELF BY HIDING AMONG THE HORSES ON THE PICKET LINE.

THE DAY OF THE TOURNAMENT DAWNS CLEAR AND BRIGHT, AND VAL, GOING TO THE HORSE LINES TO GROOM ARVAK FOR THE GAMES, FINDS HE HAS TORN LOOSE.

1-26-64

VAL LEADS ARVAK BACK TO HIS PLACE AND IS BRUSHING HIS GLOSSY FLANKS WHEN HIS EYE IS CAUGHT BY A BRIGHT OBJECT IN THE GRASS — A KNIFE!

1407

HAL FOSTER

WHO IS THIS ENEMY WHO WISHES HIM TO LOSE IN THE TOURNAMENT BY CRIPPLING ARVAK? SOMEONE WHO HAS AN EMPTY SHEATH AND, PERHAPS, SOME HOOF MARKS.

NEXT WEEK - **The Great Tournament**

Prince Valiant
IN THE DAYS OF KING ARTHUR
WRITTEN AND ILLUSTRATED BY HAROLD R. FOSTER

Our Story: LONG BEFORE SUNUP THE GROUNDS ARE CROWDED WITH NOISY TOWNSPEOPLE, VENDORS HAWK THEIR WARES, PICKPOCKETS ARE BEATEN, FIGHTS BREAK OUT, AND THE WRESTLERS, JUGGLERS AND MOUNTEBANKS BRING FORTH SHOUTS AND LAUGHTER.
THEN TO THE ROLL OF DRUMS AND THE BLARING OF TRUMPETS KING ARTHUR AND QUEEN GUINEVERE TAKE THEIR PLACES IN THE ROYAL PAVILION, AND THE PARADE OF CONTESTANTS BEGINS.

BECAUSE OF RUMORS OF IMPENDING INVASION, THE KING WANTS EVERY WARRIOR IN TOP FORM, SO PRIZES FOR THE ARCHERS, SPEAR THROWERS, SLINGERS AND SWORDS- MEN ARE DOUBLED AND TRIPLED.

THEN THE KNIGHTS CONTEND IN THE GRAND MELEE, AFTER WHICH TIME IS TAKEN OUT FOR LUNCH WHILE THE DEBRIS IS CLEARED FROM THE FIELD.

NOW COMES THE MAIN EVENT WHEN KNIGHT MEETS KNIGHT IN SINGLE COMBAT. PRINCE VALIANT TAKES HIS PLACE IN THE CHALLENGE LINE, WONDERING WHO HIS SECRET ENEMY IS.
1408

WITHOUT AS MUCH AS A 'BY YOUR LEAVE' COUNT BRECEY TAKES THE SEAT BESIDE QUEEN ALETA. AND WHY NOT? AS SOON AS HUGO KILLS SIR VALIANT, BRECEY WILL MAKE HER HIS WIFE.
2-2-64

AND HUGO MUST KILL VALIANT TO WIN THE FIEF AND CASTLE OF GLANDON THAT BRECEY HAS PROMISED HIM. HIS DEFEAT AT THE HOOFS OF THE RED STALLION HAS SHAKEN HIS CONFIDENCE, AND HIS CRACKED RIB HURTS!
NEXT WEEK— The Empty Sheath
HAL FOSTER

Prince Valiant
IN THE DAYS OF KING ARTHUR
WRITTEN AND ILLUSTRATED BY HAROLD R FOSTER

Our Story: HUGO DOES NOT JOIN IN THE TILTING. HE WATCHES PRINCE VALIANT LIKE A HAWK, TRYING TO FIND SOME WEAKNESS HE CAN TAKE ADVANTAGE OF WHEN HIS DEADLY WORK BEGINS.

AND HE NOTES SIR VALIANT'S SKILL AND ACCURACY AS HE UNHORSES ONE CHALLENGER AFTER ANOTHER. HUGO IS CONFIDENT HIS GREAT STRENGTH CAN OFFSET THAT SKILL, BUT THE HORSEMANSHIP IS A DIFFERENT STORY. THE SUPERB TRAINING AND ENERGY OF THE RED STALLION GIVE VAL A GREAT ADVANTAGE.

SOON THERE ARE BUT THREE VICTORS LEFT, SIR LAUNCELOT, GAWAIN AND VAL. IT SEEMS CERTAIN THE MIGHTY LAUNCELOT WILL ONCE AGAIN RECEIVE THE PRIZE. THEN A TRUMPET BLARES OUT A CHALLENGE.....

.... AND HUGO, SILENT AND MENACING, PACES FORWARD SLOWLY AND STRIKES VAL'S SHIELD A RINGING BLOW WITH A STEEL-TIPPED LANCE— A CHALLENGE TO MORTAL COMBAT HAS BEEN GIVEN.

KING ARTHUR IS WROTH. HE HAD NOT FORBIDDEN MORTAL COMBAT, BUT HE HAD MADE IT CLEAR THAT WAR IS IMMINENT AND HE DOES NOT WANT HIS KNIGHTS KILLED IN PLAY. BESIDES, THE CHALLENGE IS UNFAIR. HUGO IS FRESH WHILE VAL HAS FOUGHT LONG AND HARD.

ALETA SITS WHITE-FACED AND STILL. VAL CANNOT WITH HONOR REFUSE THE UNFAIR BOUT. IT SEEMS TO HER AS IF HE MUST FACE A LEGAL MURDER.

1409   2-9-64

SHE GLANCES AT COUNT BRECEY. HE IS LEANING FORWARD EAGERLY AND RUBBING HIS HANDS TOGETHER IN ANTICIPATION. OF WHAT?

NEXT WEEK— **The Duel Begins**

HAL FOSTER

Prince Valiant
IN THE DAYS OF KING ARTHUR
WRITTEN AND ILLUSTRATED BY HAROLD R FOSTER

Our Story: PRINCE VALIANT AND HUGO PRESENT THEMSELVES BEFORE THE ROYAL PAVILION, AND THE GRAND MARSHAL REPEATS THE RULES GOVERNING MORTAL COMBAT.

IN THE CENTER OF THE LISTS THE TWO COMBATANTS SALUTE EACH OTHER...ONE FOR THE LAST TIME. THEN THEY RETIRE TO ARM THEMSELVES FOR THE TRIAL. DURING THE NIGHT SOMEONE TRIED TO CRIPPLE ARVAK AND DROPPED HIS KNIFE, AND HUGO HAS AN EMPTY SHEATH AND A HOOFMARK ON HIS JERKIN.

THERE ARE STRICT RULES AGAINST STRIKING A MOUNT IN COMBAT, BUT HUGO HAS PROVED THAT HE OBEYS NO LAWS. VAL COVERS ARVAK'S NECK AND WITHERS WITH PROTECTIVE ARMOR AND GRASPS HIS DEADLY STEEL-TIPPED LANCE.

ON THE FIRST THUNDERING CHARGE BOTH LANCES ARE SHATTERED. VAL SHAKES LOOSE THE KEEN LANCE POINT EMBEDDED IN HIS LIGHT SHIELD AND DRAWS THE 'SINGING SWORD'!

HOW HUGO CURSES THE RED STALLION! NO MATTER HOW HE MANEUVERS, ARVAK STICKS TO HIS RIGHT FLANK, FORCING HIM TO TWIST IN THE SADDLE AND FIGHT OFF BALANCE.

2-16-64

COUNT BRECEY GAZES AT HIS BRIDE-TO-BE, FULLY CONFIDENT THAT HIS MIGHTY COUSIN, HUGO, WILL SOON MAKE HER A WIDOW. HOW FAIR SHE IS.....AND HIS FUTURE STEPCHILDREN ARE OF ROYAL BLOOD, TO BE MARRIED OFF TO KINGS AND QUEENS!

NEXT WEEK— **The Hoofmark**

1410

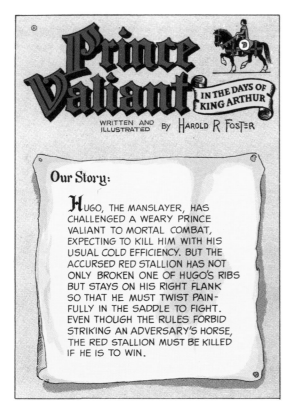

Prince Valiant
IN THE DAYS OF KING ARTHUR
WRITTEN AND ILLUSTRATED BY HAROLD R FOSTER

Our Story:

HUGO, THE MANSLAYER, HAS CHALLENGED A WEARY PRINCE VALIANT TO MORTAL COMBAT, EXPECTING TO KILL HIM WITH HIS USUAL COLD EFFICIENCY. BUT THE ACCURSED RED STALLION HAS NOT ONLY BROKEN ONE OF HUGO'S RIBS BUT STAYS ON HIS RIGHT FLANK SO THAT HE MUST TWIST PAIN-FULLY IN THE SADDLE TO FIGHT. EVEN THOUGH THE RULES FORBID STRIKING AN ADVERSARY'S HORSE, THE RED STALLION MUST BE KILLED IF HE IS TO WIN.

SLIPPING HIS SHIELD ASIDE, HUGO GRASPS HIS SWORD IN BOTH HANDS AND AIMS A MIGHTY BLOW, NOT AT VAL'S HEAD, BUT AT THE EDGE OF HIS SHIELD. THE STROKE GLANCES OFF, AS WAS INTENDED, AND BRINGS ARVAK TO HIS KNEES.

THE HOOF MARK! HUGO'S MOUTH OPENS IN A GASP OF PAIN AS THE SWORD POINT FINDS ITS MARK, AND THE FRACTURED RIB BENEATH IT CAVES IN.

BLIND WITH PAIN HUGO FUMBLES FOR THE GRIP ON HIS SHIELD. FOR AN INSTANT HIS NECK IS EXPOSED, THE 'SINGING SWORD' FLASHES OUT, AND THE FIGHT IS OVER.

IN ONE LAST FLASH OF HATRED HUGO STRIVES TO REACH THE HORSE THAT HAS CAUSED HIS FIRST AND ONLY DEFEAT. THEN DARKNESS COMES.

NO ONE COULD GUESS THE AGONY ALETA HAS SUFFERED DURING THE LONG HOUR OF COMBAT AS SHE RISES SO CALMLY TO WAVE TO THE VICTOR.
LANCELOT AND GAWAIN RETIRE FROM THE TOURNAMENT, AND FOR THE FIRST TIME SINCE COMING TO CAMELOT, PRINCE VALIANT IS CROWNED GRAND CHAMPION.

COUNT BRECEY LOOKS AT ALETA WITH BURNING EYES. NOW JEALOUSY IS ADDED TO DESIRE. SOME DAY HE WILL MAKE HER LOOK AT HIM THUS!

NEXT WEEK — **The Abduction**

HAL FOSTER

2-23-64

1411

Prince Valiant
IN THE DAYS OF KING ARTHUR
WRITTEN AND ILLUSTRATED BY HAROLD R FOSTER

Our Story: FOR THE FIRST TIME PRINCE VALIANT IS ACCLAIMED CHAMPION OF THE GRAND TOURNAMENT, AND THE CHAPLET OF VICTORY IS PLACED ON HIS LANCE TIP. THIS BAUBLE HE PRESENTS TO ALETA AS HIS CHOICE OF QUEEN OF BEAUTY. AFTER SEEING HIM SLAY THE MIGHTY HUGO IN MORTAL COMBAT NO ONE DISPUTES HIS CHOICE.

VAL DISMOUNTS STIFFLY AND CALLS HIS SQUIRES TO REMOVE THE COIF FROM ARVAK'S NECK. THE LEATHER AND CHAIN MAIL STAYED HUGO'S MIGHTY STROKE, BUT THE WITHERS ARE BADLY BRUISED AND SWOLLEN.

KNOWING THAT VAL WILL STAY UNTIL ARVAK HAS RECEIVED THE BEST OF CARE, ALETA AND ARN HASTEN HOME TO PREPARE THE SALVES, OINTMENTS AND BANDAGES HE WILL NEED.

COUNT BRECEY SEETHES WITH ANGER. THESE STUPID BRITONS DO NOT SEEM TO REALIZE THAT HE MUST HAVE WHAT HE DESIRES. IN HIS OWN FIEF, WHERE HE HAS THE POWER OF LIFE AND DEATH, HIS PEOPLE UNDERSTAND MUCH BETTER.

HE ORDERS HIS RETAINERS TO HORSE. THEY WERE PREPARING TO BURY HUGO, BUT AS HUGO FAILED TO KILL SIR VALIANT AND MAKE ALETA A WIDOW, HE IS USELESS NOW... AND THERE IS OTHER WORK TO BE DONE.

ARN IS KNOCKED FROM HIS MOUNT, ALETA IS SEIZED AND THROWN ON A HORSE, AND BRECEY AND HIS RETAINERS GALLOP AWAY FROM CAMELOT IN THE GATHERING DUSK ON THEIR WAY TO SEA.

1412

"TELL SIR VALIANT THAT QUEEN ALETA HAS BEEN ABDUCTED BY COUNT BRECEY!" AND ARN MOUNTS AND RIDES IN PURSUIT.

NEXT WEEK—'The Hornet'

3-1-64

Our Story: THE TOURNAMENT IS OVER AND PRINCE VALIANT LEAVES HIS WAR HORSE, ARVAK, IN THE HANDS OF THE HOSTLERS AND HIS BATTERED ARMS WITH THE ARMORER. WEARILY HE MOUNTS HIS SPARE HORSE.

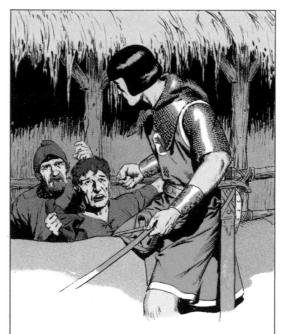

"THE LADY ALETA HAS BEEN STOLEN!" GASP THE TWO LITTER BEARERS. "COUNT BRECEY IS RIDING WITH HER TOWARD THE SEA, PRINCE ARN IN PURSUIT."

BUT THE FAIR ALETA IS GIVING TROUBLE. SHE NEARLY BLINDS THE MAN WHO CARRIES HER, WRIGGLES OUT OF HIS GRASP, AND FALLS TO THE GROUND.

SHE RUNS, BUT THEY RIDE HER DOWN AND THIS TIME TIE HER SECURELY BEHIND THE RIDER. SHE SEEMS QUIET BUT IS ONLY REACHING FOR THE KEEN LITTLE DAGGER SHE CARRIES IN HER GARTER.

CUTTING HERSELF LOOSE, SHE APPLIES HER SMALL WEAPON WITH SUCH EFFICIENCY THAT THE MAN TUMBLES SCREAMING FROM THE SADDLE. THEN ALETA SEIZES THE REINS AND TURNS FROM THE ROAD.

ARN HALTS AS THE MOON COMES OUT, FLOOD-ING THE SCENE WITH LIGHT, AND SEES HIS MOTHER BEING LED BACK TO THE ROAD WITH HER FEET TIED UNDER THE HORSE.

1413

AS THEY CLATTER AWAY ARN IS TRYING TO FIND A PLAN BY WHICH AN UNARMED BOY CAN RESCUE A LADY FROM THE FIVE REMAINING SOLDIERS, WHEN HE HEARS A RIDER COMING UP BEHIND HIM.

VAL RIDES UP, UNARMED SAVE FOR THE 'SINGING SWORD.' "WHOA, FATHER," CALLS ARN CHEERFULLY. "MOTHER HAS LEFT SHIELD AND HELMET FOR YOU IN YONDER DITCH. WE MUST HURRY ERE SHE DESTROYS THE REST OF THEM!"

NEXT WEEK— Arn to the Rescue

3-8-64

Prince Valiant
IN THE DAYS OF KING ARTHUR
WRITTEN AND ILLUSTRATED By HAROLD R FOSTER

Our Story: IT IS JUST AS ARN HAS SAID. ALETA HAS LEFT VAL A SHIELD AND HELMET. THE OWNER GIVES THEM UP WILLINGLY, FOR HE HAS BEEN SLASHED, STABBED AND THROWN FROM HIS HORSE BY A SMALL BLONDE, AND IT HAS SHAKEN HIS CONFIDENCE.

FATHER AND SON RESUME THEIR PURSUIT. "SIRE, I HAVE NO ARMS OR ARMOR, AND THERE ARE FIVE OF THEM AGAINST US, BUT........." AND ARN UNFOLDS A PLAN.

ARN, LIGHT IN THE SADDLE, SOON OVERTAKES HIS MOTHER'S ABDUCTORS. "HALT!" HE CRIES. "'TIS I, PRINCE ARN, TO THE RESCUE!" COUNT BRECEY ORDERS ONE OF HIS RETAINERS: "RID ME OF THIS NUISANCE."

THE LOUD 'NUISANCE' SEEMS TO LOSE HIS COURAGE AND RETREATS BEFORE THE SOLDIER'S CHARGE..... RETREATS WITHIN REACH OF THE 'SINGING SWORD', AND SOON HE ALSO HAS SWORD AND SHIELD.

BRECEY SETS A SLOWER PACE THAT HIS HENCHMAN MAY CATCH UP. AND ALETA, DISHEVELLED, PALE WITH WEARINESS, GLARES AT HIM WITH SUCH CONTEMPT THAT HE WONDERS IF HE CAN EVER BREAK HER SPIRIT.

3-15-64   1414

HE CHANGES HIS TACTICS. "I LOVE YOU," HE DECLARES. "COME WITH ME AND I WILL GIVE YOU EVERYTHING YOU DESIRE." "I ONLY WANT A MAN I CAN LOVE AND RESPECT, AND YOU ARE NOT THAT MAN!" SHE ANSWERS.

HE RAISES HIS HAND TO STRIKE HER, WHEN THERE IS ANOTHER INTERRUPTION: "'TIS I, PRINCE ARN, TO THE RESCUE, AND THIS TIME SEND BACK A BETTER MAN!"

NEXT WEEK— **A Tight Rein**

Our Story: ONCE AGAIN THE FAMILIAR CRY, "*TIS I, PRINCE ARN, TO THE RESCUE!*" BRECEY, IN A RAGE, ORDERS HIS BEST GUARD, "*BRING ME THAT BRAT'S HEAD, OR I'LL HAVE YOUR OWN!*"

THE WARRIOR DRAWS HIS SWORD AND CHARGES THE NIMBLE YOUTH. "*FASTER, ARN! RIDE FASTER!*" CRIES ALETA AS HER SON CANTERS SLOWLY AWAY.

AS ARN REACHES THE TOP OF A SMALL RISE HIS PURSUER IS ALMOST UPON HIM. THEN THE DAWN LIGHT GLEAMS ON A STEEL HELMET......

.... AND PRINCE VALIANT COMES CHARGING OVER THE HILL. HE CATCHES A BLOW ON HIS SHIELD, THE 'SINGING SWORD' FLASHES, AND HE COMES THUNDERING ON.

"*TO ME!*" BELLOWS BRECEY TO HIS TWO REMAINING GUARDS. BUT THREE OF THEIR NUMBER HAVE BEEN LEFT IN VARIOUS DITCHES AND THE KNIGHT WITH THE GLEAMING SWORD SEEMS QUITE UNFRIENDLY. THEY TURN AND RACE RIGHT OUT OF THE STORY.

BRECEY CURSES THE DAY HE EVER CAME TO BRITAIN. THESE CLODS DO NOT SEEM TO UNDERSTAND THAT HE SHOULD NOT BE THWARTED. WRAPPING THE REINS OF ALETA'S MOUNT AROUND HIS HAND, HE DRAWS HIS SWORD: "*HARM ME AND THE WENCH DIES!*"

3-22   1415

ARN CALMLY REMOVES HIS HELMET, THEN, WITH A SUDDEN SHOUT, HURLS IT VICIOUSLY AT THE HORSE'S HEAD, CAUSING IT TO SHY IN TERROR.

"*SIR BRECEY, YOUR DESIRE TO MAKE OFF WITH MY WIFE IS A SINCERE COMPLIMENT TO HER BEAUTY AND MY GOOD TASTE, BUT SUCH PILFERING IS FROWNED UPON HEREABOUTS AND MERITS CORRECTIVE MEASURES.*"

NEXT WEEK— **Labor Troubles**

Our Story: PRINCE VALIANT PUTS ASIDE SHIELD AND HELMET. *"NOW WE ARE EQUALLY ARMED, BRECEY. LET US SEE IF YOU RAISE YOUR SWORD AGAINST A MAN AS READILY AS YOU FLOURISHED IT BEFORE A WOMAN."* BRECEY HAS FOUGHT IN MANY BATTLES BUT ALWAYS SURROUNDED BY HIS CHAMPIONS. NOW HE FEELS ALONE AND DEFINITELY FRIENDLESS.

"I AM THE AMBASSADOR OF KING BAN OF BRITANNY, WHOSE SON IS THE MIGHTY SIR LANCELOT. I DEMAND A FAIR TRIAL!"

SIR LANCELOT HAS A SAD DUTY TO PERFORM. ONE OF HIS BEST YEOMEN HAS BEEN SENTENCED TO THE BLOCK FOR KILLING THREE MEN IN A TAVERN BRAWL, AND HE AND GAWAIN MUST WITNESS THE EXECUTION.
JUST THEN VAL RIDES UP WITH BRECEY BOUND IN THE SADDLE AND TELLS OF HIS EVIL DEED.

"WITH THE SAXONS MARSHALING FOR WAR WE NEED EVERY HARDY FIGHTING MAN. WAS THIS YEOMAN CONDEMNED BY THE KING'S JUSTICE?" ASKS VAL. *"NO, BY THE VILLAGE SHERIFF,"* ANSWERS LANCELOT. *"THEN WE, AS THE KING'S CAPTAINS, HAVE SUPERIOR AUTHORITY,"* EXCLAIMS GAWAIN.

"LEAVE CAMELOT, GO NORTHWARD AND, WHEN THE ARMY MARCHES, JOIN MY WAR BAND. THREE SLAIN SAXONS WILL MERIT YOU A PARDON."

THEY ARE NOW CONFRONTED WITH LABOR TROUBLES. THE HEADSMAN AND GRAVE-DIGGERS CLAIM THEY ARE PAID FOR THEIR WORK AND THEY ARE BEING DEPRIVED UNJUSTLY OF THEIR INCOME.

SO, IN THE INTEREST OF GOOD LABOR RELATIONS, BRECEY IS ENTRUSTED TO THEIR CARE AND EVERYONE IS HAPPY, WITH ONE EXCEPTION.

NEXT WEEK— **Instant Justice**

1416   3-29-64

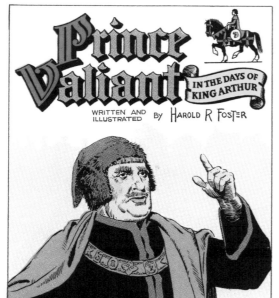

Prince Valiant
IN THE DAYS OF KING ARTHUR
WRITTEN AND ILLUSTRATED BY HAROLD R FOSTER

Our Story: THE MAGISTRATE OF CAMELOT TOWN BRINGS A GRIEVANCE TO THE KING. HE HAS ORDERED THE EXECUTION OF A TROUBLESOME RASCAL, AND SOME KNIGHTS HAVE INTERFERED WITH THE COURSE OF JUSTICE.

THE GUILTY KNIGHTS ARE SUMMONED AND THE KING CALLS FOR AN EXPLANATION. SIR LANCELOT ANSWERS: *"THE CONDEMNED MAN IS GYLES, ONE OF MY BRAVEST YEOMEN. HE SLEW THREE VAGABONDS IN A TAVERN BRAWL. I BANISHED HIM UNTIL THE FIGHTING BEGINS."*
"WE DID BUT SUBSTITUTE A MORE WORTHY CUSTOMER FOR THE HEADSMAN'S AXE," ADDS SIR GAWAIN.

"AND WHO IS THIS 'SUBSTITUTE'?" ASKS THE KING.
"COUNT BRECEY," REPLIES VAL. *"HE SOUGHT TO STEAL MY WIFE AND TAKE HER INTO BRITTANY. HE REFUSED TO FIGHT SO I BROUGHT HIM BACK FOR TRIAL!"*

SIR GAWAIN BECOMES ELOQUENT: *"WE GAVE THE COUNT A FAIR TRIAL, MY LIEGE, FOR HIS CRIME WAS GREAT. HAD HE ABDUCTED THE LADY ALETA INTO BRITTANY, FULL HALF YOUR KNIGHTS WOULD HAVE FOLLOWED TO RESCUE HER, AND WAR WITH BRITTANY WOULD WEAKEN OUR SUMMER CAMPAIGN AGAINST THE SAXONS!"*

"WE LEAVE IT TO LANCELOT TO MAKE PEACE WITH HIS FATHER, KING BAN OF BRITTANY. LOPPING THE HEAD OFF ONE OF HIS NOBLES IS NOT A GOOD WAY TO INSURE PEACE."

1417   4-5-64

SOON SUMMER WINDS WILL BE FAVORABLE AND SHIPS OF THE SAXONS, JUTES, DANES AND ANGLES WILL SWARM TO THE SHORES OF BRITAIN.
KING ARTHUR DRILLS HIS KNIGHTS AND FOOT SOLDIERS WITHOUT REST TO PERFECT THEM IN HIS NEW TACTICS. HIS CAPTAINS GRUMBLE; THERE WILL BE NO INDIVIDUAL HEROICS, JUST MACHINE-LIKE EFFICIENCY.
NEXT WEEK- **Distant Drums**

HAL FOSTER

Prince Valiant
IN THE DAYS OF KING ARTHUR
WRITTEN AND ILLUSTRATED BY HAROLD R FOSTER

Our Story: OUT OF THE EAST AND NORTH COME THE SAXONS. AND THE BEACHES FROM DOVER TO THE HUMBER ARE CLUTTERED WITH THEIR GEAR. A MIGHTY HOST IS GATHERING FOR THE FINAL CONQUEST OF ALL BRITAIN.

HUGH-THE-FOX, ONCE A FAMOUS OUTLAW, NOW CHIEF OF SCOUTS, KEEPS THE KING INFORMED OF THE SAXON MOVEMENTS. "IT WILL TAKE TWO MONTHS TO ASSEMBLE THE WAR BANDS AND BEGIN THE MARCH," HE REPORTS.

A CHERISHED DREAM CRUMBLES. ARTHUR HAS ALLOWED THE REMNANTS OF DEFEATED ARMIES TO REMAIN IN PEACE IF THEY MADE HOMES, TILLED THE SOIL, BUT RAISED NO FORTRESSES, HOPING THEY WOULD BECOME A PART OF BRITAIN.

BUT, HUGH REPORTS, WHEN THE WAR BANDS MARCH BY, THE OLD WARLIKE SPIRIT AWAKES AND THE SETTLERS TAKE THEIR WEAPONS AND FOLLOW. WAR AND PLUNDER ARE MORE TO THEIR LIKING THAN THE PLOW.

"THE TIME HAS COME TO CALL IN THE LEVIES. GO, EACH TO HIS OWN FIEF, AND BRING EVERY MAN AND HORSE YOU CAN ARM AND SUPPLY. GAWAIN AND SIR VALIANT, RIDE INTO CORNWALL AND ASK ITS THREE KINGS FOR THE TROOPS THEY PROMISED US WHEN THEY SWORE THE OATH OF FEALTY."

"PRINCE ARN, WE HAVE A MISSION FOR YOU TOO. GO TO NORTH WALES WHERE YOUR FRIEND, THE YOUNG KING CUDDOCK, OWES YOU A DEBT OF GRATITUDE, AND REQUEST HIS HELP."

IN THE DAWN FATHER AND SON BID EACH OTHER FAREWELL. A MOMENT OF PRIDE TO BOTH, FOR ARN IS TRUSTED WITH A MAN'S MISSION.

1418

ALETA WATCHES PROUDLY AS HER TWO MEN RIDE AWAY, BUT SHE HOLDS GALEN CLOSE AND WARM. ALL TOO SOON HE TOO WILL RIDE AWAY TO FACE PERIL.

NEXT WEEK—**The Recruiters**

4-12-64

Prince Valiant
IN THE DAYS OF KING ARTHUR
WRITTEN AND ILLUSTRATED BY HAROLD R FOSTER

Our Story: PRINCE ARN SETS OFF ON HIS MISSION TO NORTH WALES, TAKING WITH HIM THE THREE YOUNG KNIGHTS WHO WERE HIS COMPANIONS WHILE SCOUTING THE SAXONS IN WHITE HORSE VALE.

WHILE SIR VALIANT AND SIR GAWAIN, COMPANIONS ONCE MORE, RIDE LIGHT-HEARTEDLY WESTWARD TO CONVINCE THE THREE KINGS OF CORNWALL THAT THEIR PROMISE OF TROOPS SHOULD BE FULFILLED.

MANY A YOUNG KNIGHT IS WENDING HIS WAY TO CAMELOT TO JOIN IN THE EXPECTED FIGHTING, AND EACH, ACCORDING TO CUSTOM, CHALLENGES TO A JOUST. GAWAIN AND VAL KEEP IN PRACTICE AND TEACH SOME LESSONS.

PASSING THE MENDIP HILLS THEY COME TO AVALON, ITS THREE HILLS RISING FROM THE MARSHY LAKE AND THE SUN GLEAMING ON THE WALLS OF THE NEW CATHEDRAL BEING BUILT IN THE LITTLE TOWN OF GLASTONBURY.

VAL AND GAWAIN COME INTO CORNWALL RIDING ACROSS THE HIGH AND DESOLATE MOORS, FOR THERE IS EVER TROUBLE IN CORNWALL. SO THEY ARE NOT SURPRISED WHEN THEY DESCEND TO A RIVER CROSSING TO FIND A TROOP OF SOLDIERS GUARDING THE FORD.

"GOOD DAY TO YOU, BROTHERS," CALLS VAL. *"RIDING IN THIS SUN IS THIRSTY WORK THAT CALLS FOR A TANKARD OF ALE AT YONDER TAVERN. WILL YOU JOIN US?"*
SOON THE STERN GUARDSMEN BECOME MERRY DRINKING COMPANIONS AND TALK FREELY. THEY EVEN FURNISH A GUIDE TO SHOW THE WAY TO THEIR KING.

1419.

HAL FOSTER

"SO, EACH OF THE KINGS DISTRUSTS THE OTHERS AND KEEPS A GREAT ARMY AT RUINOUS COST FOR HIS PROTECTION. THEY WILL BE RELUCTANT TO OFFER ANY OF THEIR FORCES TO ARTHUR."

NEXT WEEK— **The Reluctant Kings**

4-19-64

Prince Valiant
IN THE DAYS OF KING ARTHUR

WRITTEN AND ILLUSTRATED By HAROLD R FOSTER

Our Story: PRINCE VALIANT AND SIR GAWAIN COME INTO CORNWALL TO ASK THE THREE KINGS FOR THEIR PROMISED LEVY OF SOLDIERS FOR THE COMING WAR WITH THE SAXON HORDE. THEIR GUIDE LEADS THEM TO CAERLOCH WHERE REIGNS KING GRUNDEMEDE.

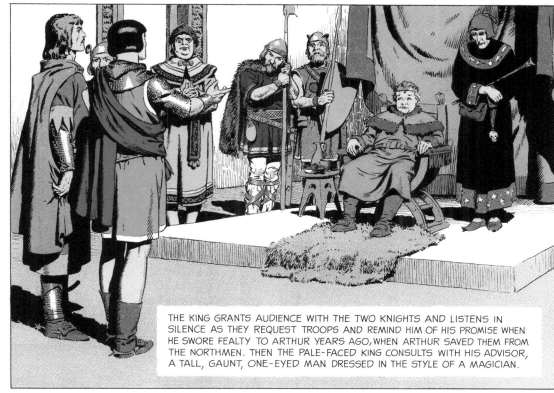

THE KING GRANTS AUDIENCE WITH THE TWO KNIGHTS AND LISTENS IN SILENCE AS THEY REQUEST TROOPS AND REMIND HIM OF HIS PROMISE WHEN HE SWORE FEALTY TO ARTHUR YEARS AGO, WHEN ARTHUR SAVED THEM FROM THE NORTHMEN. THEN THE PALE-FACED KING CONSULTS WITH HIS ADVISOR, A TALL, GAUNT, ONE-EYED MAN DRESSED IN THE STYLE OF A MAGICIAN.

"WE WILL SEND TWENTY WELL-ARMED MEN. THAT IS ALL WE CAN SPARE, FOR WE MUST PROTECT OUR COAST FROM THE RAIDING SCOTTI AND OUR BORDERS AGAINST THE THREAT OF INVASION BY THE RUTHLESS SCUM UNDER THAT TYRANT KING ALRICK-THE-FAT."

A SERF BRINGS UP THEIR SADDLEBAGS AND HE IS QUITE TALKATIVE: "THE KING ALWAYS CONFERS WITH GIVRIK, FOR HE IS A GREAT SORCERER. HE IS MASTER OF UNCOMFORTABLE MAGIC; HAS THE GIFT OF SECOND SIGHT AND POSSESSES THE EVIL EYE!"

"TO OFFER TWENTY MEN IS AN INSULT. THE OTHER TWO MONARCHS WILL FOLLOW SUIT. WE MUST HAVE TWO HUNDRED FROM EACH. THAT ONE-EYED MAGICIAN IS THE KEY FIGURE HERE."

ON THEIR WAY TO DINNER GIVRIK INTERCEPTS THEM. "BEWARE OF TRIFLING WITH THE BALANCE OF POWER HERE IN CORNWALL, OR WHAT TERRORS WILL BE YOURS IF YOU INVITE THE EVIL EYE!"

THEN HE RAISES HIS BUSHY EYEBROWS AND REVEALS A HORRID SIGHT.

NEXT WEEK— Merlin's Janitor

1420   4/26/64

Prince Valiant
IN THE DAYS OF KING ARTHUR
WRITTEN AND ILLUSTRATED BY HAROLD R FOSTER

Our Story: LIKE EVERYONE ELSE SIR GAWAIN IS SUPERSTITIOUS AND BELIEVES IN WITCHES, FAIRIES, GIANTS, DRAGONS AND ALL MANNER OF MAGIC. SO, WHEN ONE-EYED GIVRIK THE SORCERER REVEALS THE EVIL EYE, HE IS FILLED WITH FEAR.

AT DINNER GIVRIK PERFORMS MANY MIRACLES. HE PASSES HIS HAND OVER A CRYSTAL GOBLET OF WATER, AND LO, IT TURNS TO RED WINE. HIS KNIFE RISES TO HIS HAND OF ITS OWN ACCORD. TO VAL THESE ARE ALL THE CHEAP TRICKS OF FAIRGROUND ENTERTAINERS; TRICKS THAT HIS FRIEND SLITH, THE GRINNING SCOUNDREL, TAUGHT HIM TO DO YEARS AGO.

NOW, HIS OLD TEACHER, MERLIN, COULD SHOW THEM SOME REAL MIRACLES..... MERLIN! THE NAME BRINGS BACK MEMORIES. YES! THIS ONE-EYED MOUNTEBANK IS THE LAD WHO LOST AN EYE IN A BARNYARD BRAWL, AND MERLIN, OUT OF PITY, TENDED HIS WOUND AND LET HIM STAY AS A SERVANT.

WHEN THE KING, RATHER TIMIDLY, REQUESTS HIS GREAT WIZARD TO PROPHESY, VAL WATCHES INTENTLY. GIVRIK LOOKS TOWARD THE CEILING, HIS EMPTY EYE SOCKET SHOWING, AS HE MUTTERS WEIRD INCANTATIONS. HE GRIMACES AND MOANS, BUT HIS HANDS ARE FUMBLING IN HIS LAP. THEN HE BURIES HIS FACE IN HIS HANDS, AND WHEN HE LIFTS HIS FACE -- BEHOLD! THE EVIL EYE GLARES FORTH!

VAL HOPES THAT GIVRIK WILL NOT RECOGNIZE IN THE PRINCE AND KNIGHT OF TABLE ROUND, THE YOUNG PUPIL MERLIN TAUGHT SO MANY YEARS AGO.

FROM THE WEAVER'S LOOM, THE KITCHEN AND THE STABLES VAL GATHERS THE ITEMS THAT HE HOPES WILL BREAK THE POWER OF THE COURT WIZARD AND GET THE TROOPS KING ARTHUR SO SORELY NEEDS.

1421

IF THIS GAUNT, GRIM CLOWN CAN INFLUENCE THE COURT WITH THE LITTLE TRICKS HE LEARNED AS MERLIN'S JANITOR, VAL WILL SHOW THEM SOME REAL FAKING.

NEXT WEEK— **Fire from Beyond**

5-3-64

Prince Valiant
IN THE DAYS OF KING ARTHUR
WRITTEN AND ILLUSTRATED BY HAROLD R. FOSTER

Our Story: KING GRUNDEMEDE, ON THE ADVICE OF HIS WIZARD, HAS REFUSED KING ARTHUR THE TROOPS HE PROMISED. BUT WITH A FEW ODDS AND ENDS HE HAS GATHERED, VAL PLANS TO DISCREDIT THE ONE-EYED MAGICIAN.

"GIVRIK, YESTERDAY YOU TURNED WATER INTO WINE, BUT MY POWER IS GREATER—I TURN YOUR WATER TO POISON." WITH A WAVE OF HIS HAND VAL DROPS IN A FEW DYE CRYSTALS, AND BEHOLD!

WITH THE AID OF A FINE HORSEHAIR AND A BIT OF WAX, HE COMMANDS HIS KNIFE TO ARISE AND BREAK UP HIS OATCAKE.

THE PALM OF HIS HAND IS EMPTY AS HE REACHES OUT AND TAKES A GOLD COIN FROM GIVRIK'S EAR.

AGAIN THE INVISIBLE HORSEHAIR AND WAX, AND A FEATHER DANCES TO VAL'S SONG.

NOW COMES THE TEST. IN VAL'S HAND A GLITTERING COIN APPEARS AND DISAPPEARS RAPIDLY. "WATCH IT, WATCH IT!" HE COMMANDS, AND GIVRIK STARES AT IT FASCINATED WHILE VAL PLACES THE END OF A HOLLOW REED IN THE POUCH AND PRESSES THE PLUNGER, SENDING OUT ITS CHARGE OF DRY MUSTARD AND LYE.

"CHARLATAN!" SNEERS VAL, "EVEN YOUR EVIL EYE CANNOT AVAIL AGAINST MY MAGIC." GIVRIK ACCEPTS THE CHALLENGE, FOR HE HAS HAD SUCH SUCCESS WITH THAT TRICK HE ALMOST BELIEVES IT HIMSELF.

HE GOES THROUGH HIS USUAL GESTURES AND, WHEN HE REMOVES HIS HANDS, THERE IS THE BALEFUL EYE, GLEAMING.

"TOO LONG HAVE YOU USED THE POWER OF DARKNESS. NOW THE DARK GODS WILL CONSUME YOU WITH FLAMES. BURN, GIVRIK, BURN!"

1422.

A RETIRED MAGICIAN RUSHES SCREAMING FROM THE ROOM, LEAVING ONLY A PORCELAIN EYE BEHIND.
"NOW, KING GRUNDEMEDE, SHALL WE TALK ABOUT YOUR PROMISED TROOPS?"

NEXT WEEK— **The New Wizard**

5-10-64

Our Story: GIVRIK THE WIZARD DEPARTS IN UNSEEMLY HASTE, LEAVING BEHIND ONLY THE PORCELAIN EYE WITH WHICH HE HAS TERRORIZED THE COURT OF KING GRUNDEMEDE. *"HERE IS THE SO-CALLED 'EVIL EYE'!"* AND LAUGHING, PRINCE VALIANT ROLLS IT ACROSS THE TABLE. TO HIS SURPRISE, THE KING RECOILS IN HORROR FROM THE HARMLESS TRINKET.

VAL HAS USED A FEW TRICKS OF PARLOR MAGIC TO CONFOUND THE WIZARD, BUT TO HIS AMAZEMENT, HE FINDS HIMSELF REGARDED AS A GREAT SORCERER. WOULD IT BE FAIR TO CONTINUE THIS DECEPTION TO GET THE TROOPS ARTHUR SO SORELY NEEDS?

"WE CANNOT SPARE YOU THE TWO HUNDRED TROOPS YOU DEMAND. IT WOULD LEAVE US HELPLESS BEFORE THE ARMY OF KING ALRICK-THE-FAT."
"THE NUMBER IS NOW THREE HUNDRED," ANSWERS VAL, *"AND AS THEY ARE HIRED MERCENARIES, THEY WILL TURN AGAINST YOU IN REVOLT WHEN YOU CAN NO LONGER PAY THEM."*

"WE WILL MARCH, THREE HUNDRED STRONG, TO THE CASTLE OF ALRICK AND DEMAND A LIKE NUMBER FROM HIM. THUS I WILL SAVE YOU BOTH FROM BANKRUPTCY AND REBELLION."

VAL AND GAWAIN START OUT WITH AN UNDISCIPLINED MOB. FOOTSORE, WEARY, BULLIED AND DRILLED, THEY ARRIVE AT THEIR DESTINATION, BUT NOW THERE IS A SEMBLANCE OF UNITY AND EVEN PRIDE.

4123

5-17-64

ALRICK-THE-FAT LOOKS FEARFULLY FROM HIS BATTLE-MENTS AT THE APPROACHING ARMY. HIS OWN RAGTAIL GUARDS HAVE SCUTTLED BEHIND THE WALLS, WHERE THEY ARE SO CROWDED TOGETHER AS TO MAKE THEM USELESS IN CASE OF WAR.

NEXT WEEK - **Obstinate Glutton**

HAL FOSTER

Prince Valiant
IN THE DAYS OF KING ARTHUR
WRITTEN AND ILLUSTRATED BY HAROLD R FOSTER

Our Story: PRINCE VALIANT AND SIR GAWAIN BRING THEIR SMALL ARMY BEFORE THE STRONGHOLD OF ALRICK-THE-FAT AND ENCAMP IN STRICT MILITARY FASHION. TO HIS CAPTAINS VAL SAYS: "MAINTAIN A SEVERE DISCIPLINE. THESE RAGGED VAGABONDS MUST LOOK LIKE A FORMIDABLE ARMY FOR A FEW DAYS AT LEAST."

KING ALRICK IS EATING HIS WAY THROUGH THE LONG HOURS BETWEEN MEALS AND LISTENING TO THE SCOLDING OF HIS HANDSOME, COLD-EYED QUEEN. GUARDS HOLD THE TWO VISITORS AT A SAFE DISTANCE, FOR VAL'S FAME AS A MIGHTY WIZARD HAS PRECEDED HIM AND HE IS HELD IN AWE.

ALRICK, BACKED BY HIS GLOWERING SPOUSE, FLATLY REFUSES TO WEAKEN HIS FORCES. EVEN NOW, HIS AGENTS ARE TRYING TO GET SOME OF VAL'S TROOPS TO DESERT TO HIM WITH PROMISES OF BETTER PAY.

"THERE IS BUT ONE THING TO DO: GET THE THREE KINGS OF CORNWALL TO MEET TOGETHER AND SIGN A TRUCE UNTIL THE SAXON WAR IS WON. I RIDE WEST TO FETCH KING HARLOCH."

VAL RIDES WESTWARD ALONE, WHILE A MESSENGER GOES EASTWARD TO FETCH KING GRUNDEMEDE.

AND SIR GAWAIN, ALL BRUSHED, CURLED AND WAXED, MAKES HIS INDOLENT WAY TO THE SOLAR WHERE ALRICK'S QUEEN IS AT HER TAPESTRY.

IT IS NOT OFTEN THAT A HANDSOME KNIGHT VISITS THE COURT, AND SHE IS SO PLEASED THAT SHE ALMOST SMILES.

NEXT WEEK— **The Charmer**

1424   5/24/64

Prince Valiant
IN THE DAYS OF KING ARTHUR
WRITTEN AND ILLUSTRATED BY HAROLD R FOSTER

Our Story: THERE ARE THREE KINGS OF CORNWALL. EACH FEARS THE OTHERS, AND TWO OF THEM HAVE RAISED SUCH HUGE ARMIES FOR DEFENSE THAT THEY ARE BANKRUPT. PRINCE VALIANT RIDES WESTWARD TO MEET THE THIRD.

VAL CASTS PRACTICED EYES ABOUT THE COURT-YARD AND NODS APPROVAL; EFFICIENT DEFENSES, A SMALL GARRISON OF PROUD WARRIORS. KING HARLOCH MUST BE OF A DIFFERENT STRIPE FROM THOSE OTHER FRIGHTENED KINGS.

THE YEARS HAVE BENT THE BROAD SHOULDERS AND ROBBED HIS GREAT HANDS OF STRENGTH, BUT THE KING SAYS: "I KNOW OF YOUR MISSION, SIR VALIANT, AND WILL HONOR OUR PROMISE TO KING ARTHUR. MY SON, PRINCE CHARLES, WILL LEAD OUR LEVY."

"WE CANNOT OFFER MUCH IN NUMBER, BUT OURS ARE PICKED WARRIORS, STAUNCH IN BATTLE, WHO TWICE HAVE SCATTERED THE MERCENARY MOB KING ALRICK CALLS HIS 'ARMY!'"

MEANWHILE, SIR GAWAIN BEGINS HIS DAY'S WORK: "HOW IS IT, FAIR LADY, THAT YOU HAVE NEVER GRACED THE MERRY HALLS OF CAMELOT? I CAN PICTURE YOU GOWNED IN SHIMMERING CRIMSON, ORNAMENTS OF SILVER, A SINGLE ROSE IN YOUR HAIR, EARNING THE ADMIRATION OF GALLANT KNIGHTS AND THE ENVY OF FAIR WOMEN!"

"MY HUSBAND, KING ALRICK-THE-FAT, CANNOT TRAVEL, AND HAS SPENT HIS LAST PENNY MAINTAINING HIS HUGE ARMY OF UNWASHED VAGABONDS." AND SHE SIGHS.

"THEN GET RID OF THIS UNWANTED ARMY. LET ARTHUR PAY THEM INSTEAD. THEN YOU CAN AFFORD TO FOLLOW AND BE IN TIME FOR THE VICTORY CELEBRATION! CAMELOT WILL BE ABLAZE WITH LIGHT, THERE WILL BE FEASTING AND ENTERTAINMENT AND DANCING UNTIL THE DAWN!"

"YOU ARE A CHARMING LIAR, SIR GAWAIN. YOU DO NOT DECEIVE ME A BIT. I AM PLAIN AND RATHER DULL AND WILL NOT TROUBLE THE HEARTS OF GREAT WARRIORS."
THEN, FOR THE FIRST TIME IN YEARS, THE QUEEN LAUGHS: "BUT YOU HAVE WON, SIR, AND I WILL HELP YOU IF I CAN."

NEXT WEEK- **Tough Meat and Watered Wine**

1425   5-31-64

Prince Valiant
IN THE DAYS OF KING ARTHUR
WRITTEN AND ILLUSTRATED BY Harold R Foster

Our Story: SIR GAWAIN WAS NEVER MORE FASCINATING THAN WHEN HE WINS ALRICK'S QUEEN OVER TO HIS PLANS WITH FLATTERY AND PROMISES.

UP FROM THE WEST RIDES A HAPPY PRINCE VALIANT. KING HARLOCH'S LEVY ARE WELL-TRAINED VETERANS WHO WILL OFFICER THE RABBLE ARMY VAL WILL BRING TO CAMELOT, AND PRINCE CHARLES IS A CAPABLE LEADER.

AND FROM THE EAST, KING GRUNDEMEDE BOUNCES ALONG IN A HORSE LITTER, FEARFUL AND BEWILDERED.

THEY ALL COME TOGETHER IN THE HALL OF KING ALRICK-THE-FAT, WHO HAS REFUSED STEADFASTLY TO SEND THE PROMISED LEVY OF MEN TO AID KING ARTHUR. AND ALRICK IS IN A FOUL MOOD. HIS BETWEEN-MEAL SNACK IS OF WATERED WINE, TOUGH MEAT, UNSWEETENED CAKES.

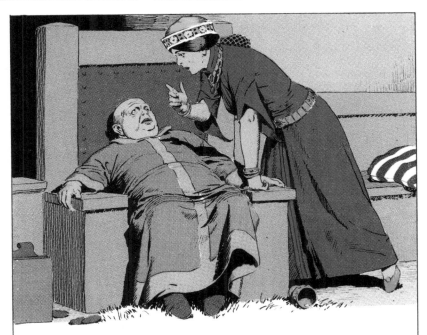

"THE FARE IS POOR," SNAPS HIS QUEEN, "AND IT WILL GET WORSE! IF YOUR FOOD IS MISERABLE, THINK WHAT YOUR ARMY MUST GET. ALREADY THEY GRUMBLE, AND REVOLT IS NEAR. WE FACE POVERTY AND FAMINE."

"NOW, WHAT COULD HAVE BROUGHT THE QUEEN OVER TO OUR SIDE?" VAL WONDERS ALOUD.
"MY DIPLOMACY, OF COURSE," SIMPERS GAWAIN. "WHAT LADY CAN RESIST MY PERSUASION?"

BUT THE QUEEN IS NOT FINISHED YET-- "AND GET THOSE UNWASHED RASCALS OUT OF OUR CASTLE. LET ARTHUR PAY AND FEED THEM!" SHE RAGES. "I RIDE TO CAMELOT FOR A VACATION. LET ME KNOW WHEN MY HOME IS FUMIGATED!"

ALRICK SITS PONDERING WHILE ONE BY ONE THE CANDLES SPUTTER AND BURN OUT. HE HAS DREAMED OF TAKING ALL CORNWALL WITH A HUGE ARMY, BUT NOW IT IS HE WHO FEARS HIS OWN ARMY MOST.
NEXT WEEK— **Always a Tomorrow**

14-26   6-7-64

Prince Valiant
IN THE DAYS OF KING ARTHUR
WRITTEN AND ILLUSTRATED BY Harold R Foster

Our Story: "BY THE AUTHORITY INVESTED IN ME BY KING ARTHUR, I HAVE DRAWN UP A TREATY. PEACE IS TO BE MAINTAINED IN CORNWALL UNTIL THE SAXON WAR IS OVER, OR THE KING'S ANGER WILL BE AROUSED."

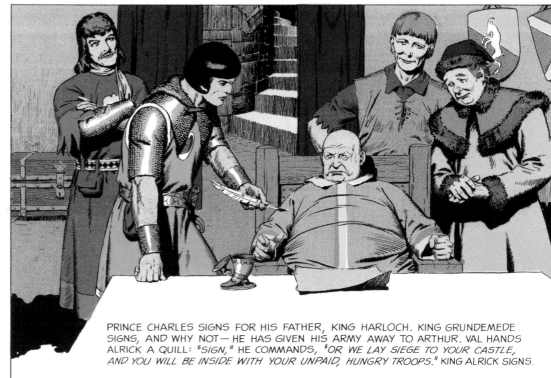

PRINCE CHARLES SIGNS FOR HIS FATHER, KING HARLOCH. KING GRUNDEMEDE SIGNS, AND WHY NOT— HE HAS GIVEN HIS ARMY AWAY TO ARTHUR. VAL HANDS ALRICK A QUILL: "SIGN," HE COMMANDS, "OR WE LAY SIEGE TO YOUR CASTLE, AND YOU WILL BE INSIDE WITH YOUR UNPAID, HUNGRY TROOPS." KING ALRICK SIGNS.

PRINCE VALIANT HAS SUCCEEDED IN RAISING AN ARMY IN CORNWALL.... BUT WHAT AN ARMY. GAWAIN, CHARLES AND A SMALL GROUP OF VETERAN WARRIORS MUST WHIP THESE VAGABONDS INTO SHAPE BEFORE THEY REACH CAMELOT.

THE STRAGGLING MOB COVERS ONLY FIVE MILES THE FIRST DAY. AT THIS RATE THEY MAY REACH CAMELOT TOO LATE. VAL CALLS HIS OFFICERS TOGETHER: "KING ARTHUR HAS SENT SUPPLIES. I HAVE ORDERED THE WAGONS PLACED TWENTY MILES APART. TELL YOUR MEN IT IS TWENTY MILES A DAY OR GO HUNGRY." THE ARMY MOVES MORE QUICKLY.

NOW OUR STORY TURNS TO PRINCE ARN, WHO HAS BEEN SENT INTO NORTH WALES TO PLEAD WITH HIS FRIEND, THE YOUNG KING CUDDOCK, FOR TROOPS TO AID ARTHUR.

1427   6-14

BUT THE BOY-KING IS NOT IN HIS STRONG-HOLD. A RAID BY THE SCOTTI HAS CALLED HIM AWAY TO THE COAST. ARN FOLLOWS.

THE SCOTTI HAVE STRUCK AND GONE AND, AS USUAL, NOT A LIVING THING STIRS AMONG THE SMOLDERING RUIN.

NEXT WEEK— Grim Tidings

Our Story: PRINCE ARN FINDS YOUNG KING CUDDOCK SURVEYING THE AWFUL RESULT OF A SCOTTI RAID. *"THEIR RAIDS HAVE INCREASED TENFOLD. HARDLY A DAY GOES BY BUT OUR LOOKOUTS REPORT THEIR SHIPS OFF OUR COASTS. THEY STRIKE AND RUN, AND IT WILL TAKE AN ARMY TO PROTECT OUR SHORES."*

WHILE THE BURIAL PARTY IS AT WORK ARN MAKES A DISCOVERY. A SAXON HELMET! CAN THIS MEAN THE SAXONS ARE ENCOURAGING THE STEPPED-UP RAIDS?

ONE OF THE YOUNG KNIGHTS OF ARN'S ESCORT HAS A SUGGESTION: *"WHY REBUILD THE VILLAGE AND TEMPT ANOTHER RAID? RATHER PUT FUEL IN THE RUINED HOUSES TO BE LIT WHEN RAIDERS APPEAR. THEY WILL NOT ATTACK A SMOLDERING RUIN."*

FORTS AND WATCHTOWERS ARE BUILT TO KEEP THE SCOTTI FROM COMING INLAND. BUT ALL THIS IS TAKING VALUABLE TIME, AND ARN IS IN DESPAIR OF GETTING THE WELSH TROOPS KING ARTHUR SO SORELY NEEDS.

A MESSENGER ARRIVES FROM CAMELOT. THE SAXON ARMY IS ON THE MOVE, A MIGHTY HOST! ARN IS TO BRING WHATEVER TROOPS HE CAN GATHER, IMMEDIATELY.

THE BOY-KING GATHERS HIS ADVISORS TOGETHER AND SAYS: *"WE BELIEVE THE SAXONS ARE AIDING THE SCOTTI RAIDERS, SO WE CANNOT GIVE AID TO ARTHUR. HOWEVER, IF HE IS DEFEATED, WE DIE OR BECOME SAXON SLAVES! WHAT DO YOU ADVISE?"*

NEXT WEEK— **The Horses**

1428   6-21

Our Story: PRINCE ARN, WITH HIS USUAL GRAVE COURTESY, LEAVES THE COUNCIL CHAMBER, THAT KING CUDDOCK AND HIS ADVISORS CAN TALK FRANKLY AND DECIDE WHETHER TO DEFEND THEMSELVES AGAINST THE SCOTTI RAIDS OR HELP KING ARTHUR.

"THE RAIDS ARE BECOMING MORE SEVERE AND WE MUST PROTECT OUR HOMELAND, BUT THE COUNCIL HAS DECIDED TO OFFER WHAT SMALL AID WE CAN TO ARTHUR."

THE DAYS DRAG ON AND ARN IS IN DESPAIR. HOW CAN HE MARCH THE LONG MILES AND REACH THE BATTLEFIELD IN TIME? THEN DESPAIR TURNS TO JOY.

FROM THE GREEN HILLS AND LUSH MEADOWS COME THE HORSES THAT ARE THE PRIDE OF THE KINGDOM, SURE-FOOTED, SWIFT AND WELL-TRAINED!

"THE WARRIORS ARE FINE HORSEMEN AND EACH WILL LEAD TWO SPARE MOUNTS. MAYBE WE CAN FILL THESE SADDLES WITH RECRUITS ON OUR WAY, FOR I RIDE WITH YOU TO MY FIRST BATTLE!"

SWIFT AS THEY RIDE, THE DAYS SEEM TO PASS EVEN MORE QUICKLY. THE YOUNG KING FEARS HE WILL ARRIVE TOO LATE FOR HIS FIRST TASTE OF WAR.

IT IS ABOUT THIS TIME THAT PRINCE VALIANT ARRIVES AT CAMELOT WITH THE CORNWALL LEVY. "GAWAIN, VAL!" CRIES ARTHUR, "WE FEARED YOU WOULD NOT ARRIVE IN TIME. THE SAXON HOST IS ON THE MARCH AND THEIR NUMBERS ARE AS THE SANDS OF THE SHORE. WE ARE READY TO RIDE TO OUR CHOSEN BATTLEGROUND."

NEXT WEEK— **Marching Armies**

1429

6-28

Prince Valiant
IN THE DAYS OF KING ARTHUR
WRITTEN AND ILLUSTRATED BY HAROLD R FOSTER

Our Story: HENGIST BEGINS HIS MARCH AND THE VERY GROUND TREMBLES UNDER THE TREAD OF HIS MIGHTY ARMY. NO PLUNDERING RAID THIS, BUT A SUPREME EFFORT TO CONQUER BRITAIN. FAIR LANDS STRETCH BEFORE THEM, A BLACKENED DESERT BEHIND.
FOR A YEAR HENGIST HAS BEEN PLANNING, GATHERING IN THE WAR BANDS AND SPYING OUT HIS ROUTE. IN THIS HE HAS BEEN LUCKY. A VIKING LAD HAS SHOWN HIS SCOUTS THE PERFECT WAY INTO THE COUNTRY'S HEART-LAND.

AND THAT VIKING LAD HAD BEEN ARN, SON OF SIR VALIANT. HE HAD SHOWN THE SAXONS THE ROUTE UP THE THAMES VALLEY AND THROUGH THE WHITE HORSE VALE. NOW THAT KING ARTHUR KNOWS WHERE TO EXPECT THE ATTACK, HE CAN CHOOSE AND PREPARE HIS OWN BATTLEGROUND.

NOW ARTHUR FASTENS HIS SWORD, EXCALIBUR, TO HIS BELT AND MOUNTS HIS GREAT WAR HORSE. THE TIME HAS COME TO PIT HIS SMALL ARMY OF PROUD WARRIORS AGAINST THE SAVAGE HORDE OF SAXONS.

AND THE SITE HE HAS CHOSEN TO DO BATTLE IS BADON HILL, WHERE PRINCE ARN HAD HIS ADVENTURE WITH THE SAXON SCOUTS. HERE ARTHUR AND HIS CHIEFTAINS PLAN THEIR STRATEGY AND PREPARE THE FIELD.

1430

7-5-64

HAL FOSTER

FROM NORTH WALES, RIDING HARD, COME ARN AND YOUNG KING CUDDOCK WITH A TROOP OF HORSEMEN HOPING TO ARRIVE IN TIME, FOR ARTHUR WILL NEED EVERY SWORD AND SPEAR.
NEXT WEEK- **The Last Reserves**

Prince Valiant

IN THE DAYS OF KING ARTHUR

WRITTEN AND ILLUSTRATED By HAROLD R FOSTER

Our Story: THE SETTING SUN GLEAMS ON HORNED HELMETS AND SPEAR POINTS AS THE SAXON HORDE AT LAST APPEARS, FILLING THE VALE WITH ITS VAST NUMBERS. AS NIGHT FALLS, A THOUSAND CAMPFIRES FLICKER IN THE DARKNESS. SUCH A HOST HAS NEVER BEFORE MARCHED ON BRITAIN.

AT DAWN BATTLE LINES ARE FORMED, AND HENGIST, KNOWING HE CANNOT HOLD BACK HIS SAVAGE WARRIORS, SENDS THEM SHOUTING TOWARDS THEIR WAITING FOES.

ARTHUR'S FOOT SOLDIERS FORM IN THREE LINES ACROSS THE VALLEY FLOOR. EVERY QUARTER-HOUR A TRUMPET SOUNDS AND THE FIRST LINE STEPS BACK AND THE LINE BEHIND TAKES ITS PLACE. THE SAXONS, HAMPERED BY THEIR OWN NUMBERS, MUST ALWAYS FACE FRESH TROOPS.

"SIR VALIANT, THE RIGHT WING IS GIVING WAY. TAKE YOUR TROOP AND RELIEVE THE PRESSURE!"
"GAWAIN, THE SAXONS ARE SWARMING OUT OF THE VALE AND WILL GET TO OUR REAR. DRIVE THEM BACK!"

"AND NOW, LANCELOT, IT IS OUR TURN. SEE, THE HORSETAIL STANDARD OF HENGIST IS ADVANCING TOWARD OUR STANDARD. HE WANTS TO CONTEND WITH ME PERSONALLY AND SHOULD NOT BE KEPT WAITING."

ALL OF ARTHUR'S FORCES ARE NOW COMMITTED TO THE BATTLE AND IT IS WIN OR DIE, FOR THERE ARE NO RESERVES TO CALL ON .... UNLESS ....

HAL FOSTER

.... THE SMALL TROOP PRINCE ARN BROUGHT FROM WALES CAN BE COUNTED UPON. AND THEY ARE STILL FAR AWAY, BUT RACING TOWARD THE DISTANT ROAR OF BATTLE.

NEXT WEEK— The Gamble

1431   7-12-64

Prince Valiant
IN THE DAYS OF KING ARTHUR
WRITTEN AND ILLUSTRATED BY HAROLD R FOSTER

Our Story: THE BATTLE OF BADON HILL ROARS TO ITS PEAK AND THE FATE OF A NATION HANGS IN THE BALANCE. PRINCE VALIANT FEELS AGAIN THE SAVAGE ECSTASY OF COMBAT AS HE LEADS HIS TROOP AGAINST THE SAXONS WHO ARE ENCIRCLING THE RIGHT WING.

SIR GAWAIN LEADS A CHARGE THAT FORCES THE SAVAGE FOE BACK INTO THE VALE WHERE THE NUMBERS ARE SO GREAT THAT MOST OF THEM HAVE NOT BEEN ABLE TO REACH THE FIGHTING FRONT.

THE HORSETAIL STANDARD OF HENGIST NEARS THE STANDARD OF ARTHUR PENDRAGON, AND MIGHTY DEEDS ARE DONE WHEN THE HARDIEST WARRIORS OF BOTH SIDES CONTEND FOR VICTORY.

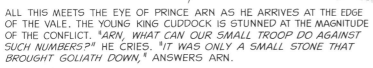

ALL THIS MEETS THE EYE OF PRINCE ARN AS HE ARRIVES AT THE EDGE OF THE VALE. THE YOUNG KING CUDDOCK IS STUNNED AT THE MAGNITUDE OF THE CONFLICT. "ARN, WHAT CAN OUR SMALL TROOP DO AGAINST SUCH NUMBERS?" HE CRIES. "IT WAS ONLY A SMALL STONE THAT BROUGHT GOLIATH DOWN," ANSWERS ARN.

THE FOOT SOLDIERS ARE STILL HOLDING THE SHIELD-WALL ACROSS THE VALLEY FLOOR, BUT NOW THEIR THREE LINES ARE REDUCED TO TWO. STEP BY STEP THEY RETREAT, LEAVING THE DEAD AND WOUNDED TO HAMPER THE STEPS OF THE SAXONS. NOW THE SAXONS SPREAD OUT AND THREATEN TO ENGULF THE LEFT WING.

"THERE IS OUR TARGET!" SHOUTS ARN, POINTING. CHARGING DOWNHILL, KING CUDDOCK IS IN THE MIDST OF HIS FIRST BATTLE.

"SIRE, THE LINE IS CRUMBLING UNDER THE PRESSURE OF NUMBERS," BELLOWS LANCELOT. "SO I SEE," ANSWERS ARTHUR. "SOUND THE TRUMPETS AND CALL ALL THE MOUNTED KNIGHTS TO OUR STANDARD. WE MUST GAMBLE ALL ON ONE CAST OF THE DICE."

NEXT WEEK— The Seeds of Panic

1432   7-19-64

Prince Valiant
IN THE DAYS OF KING ARTHUR
WRITTEN AND ILLUSTRATED BY Harold R Foster

Our Story: KING ARTHUR SIGNALS HIS TRUMPETER, AND THE RALLYING CALL RINGS OUT, BRINGING THE SURVIVING KNIGHTS TO THE STANDARD.

HENGIST, SURROUNDED BY HIS EARLS AND FIERCEST WARRIORS, REACHES THE TOP OF BADON HILL WHERE ARTHUR AND HIS PICKED KNIGHTS AWAIT HIM. POETS AND TROUBADORS STILL TELL OF THE MIGHTY DEEDS THAT TOOK PLACE THAT DAY.

FROM THE HILLTOP HENGIST LOOKS DOWN. ALTHOUGH HIS WARRIORS OUTNUMBER ARTHUR'S TWENTY TO ONE, THEY ARE BEING CONTAINED ON THE VALLEY FLOOR IN A STRUGGLING MASS. ONLY THE FRONT LINE CAN STRIKE A BLOW!

PRINCE VALIANT AND HIS COMPANIONS-AT-ARMS HAVE SAVED THE RIGHT WING, WHEN THE TRUMPET CALLS THEM TO THE STANDARD. BUT WHAT OF THE LEFT WING? HE GLANCES BACK. A TROOP OF WILD-RIDING HORSEMEN COME STORMING DOWN THE SLOPE AND SCATTER THE ENVELOPING SAXONS. WHO ARE THEY?

HENGIST MUST GET HIS WARRIORS OUT OF THE VALE AND BEHIND THE SHIELD WALL. HIS MEN SEE THE HORSETAIL STANDARD RACING DOWN THE HILL. CAN THIS MEAN A RETREAT, ARE THEY LOSING THE BATTLE?

THEN THE KNIGHTS OF THE ROUND TABLE COME POURING OVER THE CREST OF BADON HILL IN A GLITTERING FLOOD. INTO THE TIGHTLY-PACKED SAXONS THEY CRASH AT AN ANGLE, SLICING OFF SMALL SECTIONS.

1433

7-26-64

AND THESE GROUPS, TOO SMALL TO CONTEND WITH MOUNTED KNIGHTS, RUN FOR SAFETY. THE SEEDS OF PANIC ARE SOWN.

NEXT WEEK— *Victory at Badon Hill*

Prince Valiant

IN THE DAYS OF KING ARTHUR

WRITTEN AND ILLUSTRATED BY HAROLD R FOSTER

Our Story: KING ARTHUR RIDES TO THE KNOLL OVERLOOKING THE BATTLEFIELD, TAKING WITH HIM HIS TRUMPETERS AND A FEW MESSENGERS. FROM THERE HE DIRECTS THE BATTLE.

THE MIGHTY KNIGHTS OF THE ROUND TABLE FORM THE TERRIBLE WEDGE AND, LIKE A PLOWSHARE, CUT A CRIMSON PATH THROUGH THE PRESS, LOPPING OFF SMALL DETACHMENTS.

IT IS PRINCE VALIANT'S TASK TO CHARGE THESE GROUPS AND SCATTER THEM IN PANIC.

THE VAST MAJORITY OF THE SAXON HORDE HAVE STRUGGLED ALL DAY TO REACH THE FIGHTING FRONT. CRUSHED TOGETHER, UNABLE TO MOVE, THEY WATCH AS THE KNIGHTS SLICE EVER CLOSER AS ONE WOULD PEEL AN ONION. PANIC BEGINS TO SWEEP THROUGH THEM.

AND PANIC IS A STRANGE MADNESS. BOLD WARRIORS WHO WOULD FACE DEATH IN BATTLE WITHOUT FEAR DROP THEIR WEAPONS AND RUN LIKE FRIGHTENED RABBITS.

TWO YOUNG WARRIORS LEAVE THE FIELD. BOTH ARE BLEEDING FREELY FROM VERY SATISFACTORY BATTLE WOUNDS. HOW PROUD THEY ARE!

HENGIST MIGHT HAVE RE-FORMED FOR A COUNTERATTACK, BUT THE CAMP FOLLOWERS, COOKS, SERVANTS AND SLAVES HAD ARRANGED THE BAGGAGE WAGONS ACROSS THE VALLEY FLOOR SO THEY COULD VIEW THE GREAT BATTLE. NOW IT IS LIKE A DAM HOLDING BACK THE FLOOD OF FUGITIVES.

NEXT WEEK—**The Wagon Train**

1434   8-2-64

Prince Valiant
IN THE DAYS OF KING ARTHUR

WRITTEN AND ILLUSTRATED BY HAROLD R FOSTER

Our Story: WHEN VICTORY IS WON THE GREAT CAPTAINS JOIN ARTHUR UNDER HIS STANDARD. THE DESTRUCTION OF A BEATEN ENEMY USUALLY IS LEFT TO LESSER KNIGHTS AND FOOT SOLDIERS. BUT THIS TIME ARTHUR SAYS: "WE HAVE TREATED THE SAXON FAIRLY, ALLOWING HIM TO MAKE A HOME ON OUR SOIL, ONLY TO HAVE HIM TURN UPON US AT EVERY OPPORTUNITY. LET US FINISH OUR WORK!"

AND SO THE PURSUIT CONTINUES AT THE WAGONS, AT RIVER CROSSINGS AND BEYOND. THOSE WHO ESCAPE THE SWORD FALL FROM HUNGER, FOR THEY HAD LAID WASTE THE COUNTRYSIDE IN THEIR ADVANCE.

"WE HAVE REACHED THE SEA, NO SAXON STANDS BEFORE US, OUR WORK IS FINISHED," ANNOUNCES ARTHUR. HENGIST HAS SOMEHOW MANAGED TO ESCAPE, BUT NOW HIS POWER IS BROKEN, AND THIRTY YEARS WILL PASS BEFORE THE SAXONS MOUNT ANOTHER INVASION.

SEVERAL YOUNG WARRIORS WHO HAVE WON HONOR ON THE FIELD OF BATTLE ARE KNIGHTED. AND ONE OF THEM IS PRINCE CHARLES WHO LED THE ARMY FROM CORNWALL.

TO BE A PRINCE AND HEIR TO A KINGDOM IS AN HONOR, BUT TO BE ONE OF ARTHUR'S KNIGHTS IS GREATER. AND MAYBE SOMEDAY HE MIGHT GAIN A SEAT AT TABLE ROUND.

1435   8-9-64

TWO WOUNDED VETERANS OF THE LATE WAR HAVE BEEN BROUGHT BACK TO CAMELOT AND RECEIVE VERY SPECIAL ATTENTION. YOUNG KING CUDDOCK HAS THE DUBIOUS HONOR OF WINNING THE AFFECTIONS OF THE TWINS, AND THIS COULD LEAD TO A MINOR DISASTER.

NEXT WEEK— **Rivals**

Prince Valiant
IN THE DAYS OF KING ARTHUR
WRITTEN AND ILLUSTRATED BY HAROLD R FOSTER

Our Story: THE BATTLE OF BADON HILL HAS BEEN A GREAT VICTORY AND ALL BRITAIN IS ASSURED OF PEACE FOR YEARS TO COME. THE BOISTEROUS VICTORS RETURN TO CAMELOT FOR FEASTING AND CELEBRATION, AND PROUDEST OF ALL IS PRINCE CHARLES, WHOSE LEADERSHIP OF THE CORNWALL LEVY HAS WON HIM KNIGHTHOOD.

THE PRICE OF VICTORY COMES HIGH, AND MANY A NEW-MADE WIDOW HAS NO HEART FOR THE GAIETY OF THE COURT.

PRINCE VALIANT BRINGS SIR CHARLES HOME WITH HIM AND FINDS ALETA BUSY NURSING TWO VETERAN WARRIORS WHO HAVE RECEIVED WAR WOUNDS. SHE IS ALSO ENTERTAINING AILIANORA.

THE FIRST PERSON SIR GAWAIN MEETS IS GAYLE, WIFE OF KING ALRICK-THE-FAT. "YOU *WHEEDLED ME WITH SWEET LIES INTO HELPING YOU RAISE AN ARMY IN CORNWALL AND PROMISED I WOULD BE QUEEN OF BEAUTY IN CAMELOT. WELL, I'VE COME, AND MY NIECE GRACE WILL PROVIDE THE BEAUTY I LACK.*"

NO MARRIED WOMAN CAN STAND SEEING A HAPPY BACHELOR WHEN THERE ARE SINGLE GIRLS AROUND. WHEN THE LADY GAYLE SEES CHARLES SHE KNOWS WHERE HER DUTY LIES.

AILIANORA IS A TALL, FAIR GIRL, DESERVING OF A HANDSOME HUSBAND. AFTER LOOKING OVER THE FIELD ALETA DECIDES SIR CHARLES IS MOST SUITABLE. ALAS, CHARLES, YOUR DAYS OF BACHELORHOOD ARE NUMBERED.

1436   8-16-64

THE TWINS, KAREN AND VALETA, HAVE NEVER SEEN ANYTHING AS BEAUTIFUL AS *CUDDOCK,* YOUNG KING OF NORTH WALES. AND HE WHO HAS BRAVELY FACED THE SAXONS QUAILS BEFORE THEIR DETERMINED CAMPAIGN.

NEXT WEEK—**The Matchmaker**

Prince Valiant
IN THE DAYS OF KING ARTHUR

WRITTEN AND ILLUSTRATED BY HAROLD R. FOSTER

Our Story: THE LADY ALETA IS TAKING HER PROTEGE, AILIANORA, TO THE PALACE WHEN A STRANGE THING HAPPENS. SIR CHARLES IS WALKING BENEATH THE GARDEN WALL AND GAYLE, A QUEEN OF CORNWALL, AND HER NIECE ARE WATCHING HIM........

...... QUEEN GAYLE LIFTS A FLOWER POT, TAKES CAREFUL AIM AND DROPS IT ON HIS HEAD. "YOU MIGHT HAVE HURT HIM," PROTESTS GRACE. "WHY DID YOU DO IT?"

"TO GET HIS ATTENTION," ANSWERS GAYLE. "NOW RUN DOWN AND APOLOGIZE, BE VERY FEMININE, SORRY, CHARMING AND JUST A TRIFLE STUPID."

"OH, SIR CHARLES, HOW CAN YOU EVER FORGIVE POOR CLUMSY LITTLE ME! COME OVER HERE TO THE STEPS SO I CAN BRUSH YOU OFF. YOU ARE SO BIG AND TALL YOU MAKE ME FEEL LIKE A HELPLESS LITTLE CHILD."

"THAT WAS A NASTY PLOT TO GAIN HIS ATTENTION. I SAW IT. BUT IT WILL DO YOU NO GOOD, HE IS GOING TO MARRY AILIANORA," SAYS ALETA.
"AND WILL YOU USE NASTY LITTLE PLOTS TOO?" ASKS GAYLE.
ALETA CONSIDERS. "YES," SHE ADMITS.
"SPOKEN LIKE A WOMAN," LAUGHS GAYLE. "WE SHOULD HAVE QUITE A CONTEST."

HER EYELASHES FLUTTER MODESTLY, HER WHITE HANDS ARE SOFT, HER HAIR LUSTROUS, AND SHE SMELLS LIKE SOME SORT OF FLOWER. HE HAS NOT BEEN THIS CLOSE TO A GIRL BEFORE, AND HIS HEAD BEGINS TO SWIM.

NOW THAT THEY KNOW HOW TO GET A MAN'S ATTENTION, THE TWINS AWAIT THE COMING OF CUDDOCK. "DON'T HIT HIM ON HIS WOUNDED HEAD," ADVISES THE GENTLE VALETA. "THAT'S ALL RIGHT, I'VE REMOVED THE POT," ANSWERS THE MATTER-OF-FACT KAREN.

1437   8-23

HAL FOSTER

"WE GOT HIS ATTENTION ALL RIGHT, BUT HE DOES NOT SEEM TO LOVE US MORE," MURMURS VALETA.
"SHOULD I THROW THE POT TOO?" KAREN WONDERS.

NEXT WEEK— **The Nymph**

Our Story: QUEEN ALETA SIZES UP HER ENTRY CAREFULLY. AILIANORA IS TALL, BLONDE AND WELL PUT TOGETHER. ATHLETIC PERHAPS, BUT NOT TOO VIVACIOUS. HER OPPONENT, ON THE OTHER HAND, IS SMALL, CUDDLY AND FULL OF GAIETY.

SHE MUST SHOW HER CANDIDATE TO HER BEST ADVANTAGE. SO ALETA TAKES THE PUZZLED AILIANORA TO THE LILY POND TO AWAIT THE PASSING OF SIR CHARLES.

CHARLES BOWS AS HE PASSES, AND THEN AN ACCIDENT OCCURS. AILIANORA FALLS INTO THE POND!

"HELP! HELP! SIR CHARLES, QUICK, TO THE RESCUE!" CHARLES GALLANTLY HELPS THE DRIPPING GIRL. HER WET HAIR GLEAMS LIKE GOLD IN THE SUNLIGHT AND HER SIMPLE GOWN CLINGS TO HER. HE LOOKS AT HER IN FRANK APPROVAL, FOR HE IS A GOOD JUDGE OF HORSEFLESH AND CAN DISCOVER NO FLAW ANYWHERE IN THIS YOUNG CREATURE.

"NOW COVER HER WITH YOUR CLOAK AND TAKE HER HOME BEFORE SHE CATCHES COLD!" OTHER EYES HAVE WATCHED THE PERFORMANCE.

"THAT WAS A SCURVY TRICK," SCOLDS GAYLE, QUEEN OF CORNWALL. "AN IMMODEST WAY TO SHOW OFF HER NICE FIGURE... I WISH I HAD THOUGHT OF THAT FIRST!"

1438

8-30

BELIEVING THEIR ELDERS KNOW ALL THE TRICKS TO WIN A MAN'S LOVE, THE TWINS AWAIT THE PASSING OF YOUNG KING CUDDOCK. VALETA SCREAMS AND TOPPLES INTO THE LILY POND.

"IF I WERE AS CLUMSY AS YOU TWO I WOULD HAVE A NURSEMAID IN ATTENDANCE AT ALL TIMES," GROWLS THE HARRIED LAD AS HE HEAVES VALETA ASHORE.

NEXT WEEK — **The War Is On**

Prince Valiant
IN THE DAYS OF KING ARTHUR
WRITTEN AND ILLUSTRATED BY HAROLD R FOSTER

Our Story: TWO MANAGERS HAVE ENTERED THEIR CONTESTANTS IN THE MATRIMONIAL SWEEPSTAKES, WITH SIR CHARLES AS THE PRIZE. ALETA IS SPONSORING HER PROTEGE, AILIANORA, WHILE QUEEN GAYLE DIRECTS THE DESTINY OF GRACE. AS THIS IS A CONTEST BETWEEN WOMEN, THE RULES OF FAIR PLAY HAVE BEEN SUSPENDED FOR THE DURATION.

ALETA ARRANGES TO HAVE SIR CHARLES TAKE AILIANORA HAWKING. SHE LOOKS BEAUTIFUL, HER CHEEKS FLUSHED, HER EYES BRIGHT WITH EXCITEMENT

QUEEN GAYLE COUNTERS BY ARRANGING A DANCE IN THE EVENING. GRACE IS FRESH AND GAY, WHILE AILIANORA IS TIRED AND A BIT SORE FROM RIDING.

ALETA REQUESTS SIR CHARLES TO INSTRUCT AILIANORA IN ARCHERY. *"I KNOW YOU ARE A GOOD ARCHER,"* ALETA TELLS THE GIRL, *"BUT DO NOT SHOW YOUR SKILL AT FIRST. LET CHARLES BELIEVE HIS INSTRUCTIONS ARE MAKING YOU A FINE BOWMAN."*

GAYLE PLAYS HER TRUMP! A PICNIC IN A SUNNY GLADE FAR FROM PRYING EYES... WELL, ALMOST. THE TWINS HAVE WATCHED THEIR ELDERS TRYING TO SNARE THE AFFECTIONS OF SIR CHARLES. SPORT AND FOOD JUST MIGHT WORK ON YOUNG CUDDOCK.

WITH A BRIGHT LURE THEY ATTRACT THE TROUT WITHIN REACH OF HIS SPEAR.

THEN THEY STUFF HIM WITH FOOD, FOR CUDDOCK, YOUNG KING OF NORTH WALES, IS THE MOST GORGEOUS THING THE TWINS HAVE EVER SEEN AND MUST BE MADE TO RETURN THEIR LOVE, WHETHER HE WANTS TO OR NOT.

TWO VICTIMS OF WOMEN'S PLOTTING COMPARE NOTES. *"HOW CAN A MAN GET RID OF TWO INSISTENT WOMEN WITHOUT BEING RUDE?"* ASKS CUDDOCK.
"OH, IT IS THE PRICE ONE MUST PAY FOR BEING ATTRACTIVE TO THE LADIES," ANSWERS THE BEMUSED CHARLES

NEXT WEEK - **The Ringer**

1439   9-6

Prince Valiant

IN THE DAYS OF KING ARTHUR

WRITTEN AND ILLUSTRATED BY HAROLD R. FOSTER

Our Story: SIR CHARLES' CONCEIT IS AT HIGH TIDE. IT SEEMS AS IF FAIR LADIES EVERYWHERE ARE VYING FOR HIS FAVOR. DRESSED IN NEW FINERY HE GOES OUT TO GIVE THEM A TREAT. HIS REASONING POWER IS AT LOW EBB.

HE IS BROUGHT DOWN FROM THE CLOUDS BY A DISDAINFUL SNIFF. TURNING, HE SEES A THIN GIRL WITH STRAIGHT RED HAIR AND MANY FRECKLES STARING AT HIM. "NOW, WHAT DID I DO TO DESERVE THAT?" HE DEMANDS.

"BECAUSE YOU ARE SUCH A SIMPLETON AS TO LET TWO DESIGNING WOMEN USE YOU AS A MATRIMONIAL PRIZE FOR THEIR WARDS. IT IS BECAUSE YOU ARE HEIR TO A THRONE, CERTAINLY NOT ON ACCOUNT OF YOUR GOOD LOOKS," SHE SNAPS.

"WHO ARE YOU TO TALK OF GOOD LOOKS?" ROARS CHARLES ANGRILY. "YOU ARE THIN AS A LANCE AND FRECKLED LIKE A RUSTY HELMET!"

"YOKEL," SHE ANSWERS, AS SHE SWINGS DOWN FROM HER PERCH AND WALKS AWAY, PROUDLY ERECT. AFTER ALL THE ATTENTION HE HAS RECEIVED FROM AILIANORA AND GRACE, THIS REBUFF HAS QUITE CUT HIM DOWN TO SIZE, A SMALL SIZE.

THEN HER SHOULDERS SAG. WITH HEAD BOWED SHE STUMBLES AWAY. "WAIT, LADY," HE CALLS, "I DID NOT MEAN TO BE SO RUDE. IF I HURT YOU I AM SORRY!"
"LET ME GO," SHE SOBS.

1440   9-13

BUT HE HAS A FIRM GRIP ON HER THIN SHOULDER AND STARES AT THE TEAR-WET, FRECKLED FACE; "BUT WHAT... WHY...?" HE STAMMERS.
"BECAUSE I LOVE YOU. I HAVE LOVED YOU SINCE YOU CAME TO CAMELOT. NOW LET ME GO, YOU HOMELY CLOWN!"

MINUTES GO BY, LONG BREATHLESS MINUTES, WHILE A WONDERFUL TRUTH BECOMES CLEAR. "WE WILL PROBABLY HAVE THE HOMELIEST CHILDREN IN ALL CORNWALL," HE ANNOUNCES. "WHAT IS YOUR NAME?"

NEXT WEEK — The Bride

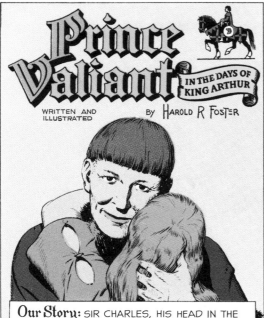

Prince Valiant
IN THE DAYS OF KING ARTHUR

WRITTEN AND ILLUSTRATED
BY HAROLD R FOSTER

Our Story: SIR CHARLES, HIS HEAD IN THE CLOUDS, HOLDS HIS NEW-FOUND TREASURE TIGHT IN HIS ARMS. THAT SHE IS THIN, RED-HAIRED AND FRECKLED MAKES NO DIFFERENCE. TO HIM SHE IS THE MOST PRECIOUS THING IN THE WORLD.

"YOU DISAPPOINT ME, SIR CHARLES," SCOLDS ALETA, "MY WARD, AILIANORA, WOULD MAKE A BEAUTIFUL ORNAMENT TO ANY COURT."
"YOU WILL RUE THIS DAY," SAYS QUEEN GAYLE DARKLY, "FOR MY NIECE WOULD MAKE A LOVELIER QUEEN THAN THAT SKINNY REDHEAD."
CHARLES LOOKS DOWN AT THE FRECKLED FACE AND GRINS: "IT SEEMS I HAVE BEEN WAITING ALL MY LIFE FOR A SKINNY REDHEAD. WILL YOU MARRY ME..... BY THE WAY, WHAT IS YOUR NAME?"

THE TWINS ARE IN DARK DESPAIR. SUFFERING FROM AN ACUTE CASE OF PUPPY LOVE FOR YOUNG CUDDOCK OF WALES, THEY HAVE COPIED THE TRICKS AND SCHEMES USED BY THEIR ELDERS TO NO AVAIL.
"GROWNUPS KNOW NOTHING OF ROMANCE," ANNOUNCES VALETA. "I WONDER HOW MOTHER EVER WON OUR SIRE!"
"SORCERY," ANSWERS KAREN, "OR MAYBE A LOVE POTION."

IF GRACE AND AILIANORA MOURN THE LOSS OF SIR CHARLES, THEY HIDE THEIR BROKEN HEARTS WELL.
"HEARTLESS WENCHES," SNEERS KAREN. "THEY SOON FORGET, WHILE OUR LOVE FOR CUDDOCK WILL LAST FOREVER "
"WE WILL ENTER A CONVENT AND EASE OUR SORROW BY DOING GOOD WORKS," ANNOUNCES VALETA.

THE DAY COMES WHEN KING CUDDOCK MUST LEAD HIS HORSEMEN BACK TO NORTH WALES. AND KAREN'S GIFT IS A DOLL'S HEAD OF WOOD, BEAUTIFULLY CARVED. VALETA'S IS A KERCHIEF: "I EMBROIDERED IT MYSELF."
"WHY DO YOU GIVE ME YOUR MOST PRECIOUS POSSESSIONS?" HE ASKS.
"BECAUSE WE LOVE YOU," IS KAREN'S POSITIVE STATEMENT.

1441   9-20

HAL FOSTER

IT IS RECORDED THAT, WHEN KING CUDDOCK RETURNED TO CAMELOT YEARS LATER TO ENTER A TOURNAMENT, HE WORE A WOODEN DOLL'S HEAD ON HIS CREST, A LADY'S KERCHIEF ON THE SHOULDER OF HIS SWORD ARM.

NEXT WEEK- *The Missing Scroll*

Our Story FALTERS, FOR ONE OF THE ANCIENT PARCHMENT SCROLLS UPON WHICH THE SAGA OF PRINCE VALIANT IS WRITTEN HAS CRUMBLED WITH AGE SO THAT THE SCHOLARS CANNOT TRANSLATE THE FINE LATIN TEXT.

BUT THE AUTHOR THINKS IT IS SAFE TO ASSUME THAT SIR CHARLES RODE WESTWARD INTO CORNWALL WITH HIS THIN, RED-HAIRED BRIDE, FIRMLY CONVINCED THAT BEAUTY IS MEASURED BY THE NUMBER OF FRECKLES.

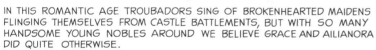

IN THIS ROMANTIC AGE TROUBADORS SING OF BROKENHEARTED MAIDENS FLINGING THEMSELVES FROM CASTLE BATTLEMENTS, BUT WITH SO MANY HANDSOME YOUNG NOBLES AROUND WE BELIEVE GRACE AND AILIANORA DID QUITE OTHERWISE.

BECAUSE OF THEIR GREAT LOVE FOR YOUNG KING CUDDOCK, THE TWINS PLAN TO ENTER A CONVENT AND DEVOTE THEIR LIVES TO DOING GOOD WORKS. BUT WE DOUBT VERY MUCH IF THEY ALLOWED THEIR SORROW TO SPOIL THEIR APPETITES OR KEEP THEM FROM THEIR NORMAL ACTIVITIES.

WHATEVER ADVENTURES WERE RECORDED ON THE DAMAGED SCROLL WE WILL NEVER KNOW, BUT WHEN THE TALE IS RESUMED, PRINCE VALIANT AND HIS FAMILY ARE ON BOLTAR'S GREAT DRAGON-SHIP HEADING NORTH AND FAR FROM SHORE. FROM THIS WE CONCLUDE THAT VAL HAS BEEN SUMMONED BY HIS FATHER, KING AGUAR OF THULE, AND DANGER LURKS ALONG THE COAST.

MIDDAY, AND THE LENGTH OF THE SHADOW CAST BY THE SUN INDICATES THAT THEY HAVE REACHED A CERTAIN LATITUDE. BOLTAR ORDERS THE SHIP TURNED TO THE EAST AND HIS MEN TO LOOK TO THEIR WEAPONS.

NEXT WEEK—Bergen

9-27-64   1442

Prince Valiant

IN THE DAYS OF KING ARTHUR

WRITTEN AND ILLUSTRATED BY HAROLD R. FOSTER

Our Story: BOLTAR SWINGS HIS DRAGONSHIP TOWARD THE MISTY COAST, AND HIS SEA ROVERS PLACE THEIR WEAPONS NEAR AT HAND AS THEY RUN OUT THE OARS.

THEY COME IN BETWEEN THE ISLANDS CAUTIOUSLY AND APPROACH THE LITTLE BOAT-BUILDING VILLAGE OF BERGEN. ANXIOUS EYES WATCH THEIR APPROACH AND ARMS ARE PLACED IN READINESS.

A MESSENGER GREETS THEM: "A HOSTILE FLEET IS MAKING ITS DESTRUCTIVE WAY UP THE COAST," HE ANNOUNCES, "AND SOMEWHERE INLAND AN ARMY MARCHES. SHOULD THE TWO UNITE AT TRONDHEIMFJORD ALL THULE WILL BE LOST."

BOLTAR AND THE ROYAL FAMILY HEAD FOR THE SAFETY OF THE OPEN SEA WHILE PRINCE VALIANT AND THE GUIDE SAIL THE INSHORE ROUTE TO THE MIGHTY SOGNEFJORD. NOW HIS GUIDE TELLS VAL OF THE DANGER THAT BESETS THULE.

"SKOGUL ODERSON HAS RECRUITED A WILD AND LAWLESS CREW FROM AMONG THE BALTIC TRIBES, LANDED THEM IN OSLOFJORD AND EVEN NOW IS MARCHING UP THE VALLEY TOWARD KING AGUAR'S STRONGHOLD."

"AT EVERY HOMESTEAD AND FARM HE GIVES HIS CAPTIVES THEIR CHOICE; SWEAR THE OATH OF LOYALTY..... OR DIE. THAT THE RUTHLESS AND CRUEL SKOGUL IS ALSO HALF MAD MAKES NO DIFFERENCE TO HIS BAND."

AT THE HEAD OF THE FJORD THEY LEAVE THE BOAT AND FOLLOW THE FJELL INLAND. THE COLD BREATH OF THE GLACIER COMES DOWN TO THEM, AND WHEN THE TATTERED RAIN CLOUDS PART THE BLUE ICE FIELD CAN BE SEEN, AND MELTING WATER STREAKS THE MOUNTAINSIDE WITH FOAMING STREAMS.

NEXT WEEK **Garm the Hunter**

HAL FOSTER

1443   10-4

Our Story: PRINCE VALIANT AND HIS COMPANION HAVE PASSED THROUGH THE COASTAL MOUNTAINS. THE GROUND NOW SLOPES AWAY. "WE ARE TO MEET A SCOUT HEREABOUTS WHO HAS INFORMATION ON THE INVASION," SAYS NALL.

VAL LOOKS AT THE VAST EXPANSE OF FORESTED HILLS WITH THEIR RIVERS, VALLEYS AND LAKES. "SKOGUL COULD HIDE HIS WHOLE WAR BAND IN THIS WILDERNESS," SAYS VAL. "HOW CAN ONE SCOUT FIND US TWO?"
"THIS IS A VERY SPECIAL SCOUT," SMILES NALL.

THEY REACH A LAKE WHERE A MAN WAITS BESIDE A BOAT, AND THE MAN LOOKS FAMILIAR. "GARM!" SHOUTS VAL, "HOW GLAD I AM TO SEE YOU AGAIN. NALL, THIS IS GARM, HUNTSMAN TO MY FATHER, THE KING, AND TEACHER OF WOODCRAFT TO MY SON, ARN."

"THIS SKOGUL ODERSON IS EITHER A GENIUS OR A MADMAN," REPORTS GARM. "HIS FLEET IS IN THE SOUTH, THREATENING RAIDS TO THE NORTHWARD. YOUR SIRE'S HARDY VIKINGS MUST BE KEPT IN READINESS TO MEET THAT THREAT. MEANWHILE SKOGUL MARCHES QUIETLY NORTHWARD. BROKEN UP INTO SMALL BANDS, HIS ARMY IS ALMOST INVISIBLE IN THIS VAST FOREST!"

FOR MANY DAYS THE THREE SCOUTS MAKE THEIR WAY SOUTHWARD, HOPING TO MAKE CONTACT WITH THE INVADING FORCES TO DETERMINE THEIR COURSE AND THEIR STRENGTH.

AT LAST THEY MEET REFUGEES FLEEING NORTHWARD IN PANIC AND TELLING TALES OF SAVAGERY THAT ARE SHOCKING EVEN IN THESE ROUGH TIMES.

SOMEWHERE OUT THERE AMID THE LAKES AND RIVERS AND FOREST-COVERED HILLS THE ENEMY IS ADVANCING LIKE A PLAGUE OF LOCUSTS, DEVOURING THE COUNTRY AS THEY GO.
NEXT WEEK- **The Equalizer**

1444   10-11

Our Story: PRINCE VALIANT TRIES TO RAISE AN ARMY TO RESIST THE FORCES OF SKOGUL, BUT ALWAYS IT IS THE SAME ANSWER: "WHY SHOULD I LEAVE ALL I HAVE TO FIGHT FOR KING AGUAR? NO! I AM OLE OLESON AND I STAY HERE AND FIGHT FOR WHAT IS MINE!"

"BOATS ARE COMING UP THE LAKE," SAYS GARM, "POSSIBLY REFUGEES WHO HAVE ESCAPED THE ENEMY."
"THEN THEY WILL HAVE LOST EVERYTHING," VAL PONDERS. "WITH NOTHING TO LOSE AND MUCH TO GAIN THEY MIGHT BE THE BEGINNINGS OF A RESISTANCE FORCE."

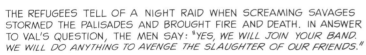

THE REFUGEES TELL OF A NIGHT RAID WHEN SCREAMING SAVAGES STORMED THE PALISADES AND BROUGHT FIRE AND DEATH. IN ANSWER TO VAL'S QUESTION, THE MEN SAY: "YES, WE WILL JOIN YOUR BAND. WE WILL DO ANYTHING TO AVENGE THE SLAUGHTER OF OUR FRIENDS."

VAL LEADS THE WAY BACK TO OLE OLESON'S STEAD. THE PALISADE IS STRONG AND THE HOUSE SERFS AND SHEPHERDS NUMBER ABOUT TWENTY STOUT MEN. BUT THE EXPECTED RAIDERS MUSTER OVER ONE HUNDRED. VAL LOOKS FOR AN EQUALIZER.

THE STREAM THAT WATERS THE FARM LOOKS PROMISING. IT WIDENS INTO A POND FILLED WITH LOGS OLE HAS CUT FOR A NEW BUILDING AND, BEST OF ALL, THE STREAM ENTERS THROUGH A NARROW CHANNEL.

ALL HANDS ARE PUT TO WORK ON A DAM THAT WILL HOLD BACK THE WATER. BY THE LIGHT OF FIRES THEY WORK THROUGH THE NIGHT, FOR VAL IS PLANNING A BATH FOR THE RAIDERS.

NEXT WEEK— *Scouts*

10-18   1445

Our Story: AT DAWN THE WEARY WORKERS HAVE THE DAM FINISHED AND THE WATER IS CREEPING UP SLOWLY BEHIND IT, MAKING A BIG RESERVOIR. A TRIGGER WILL PULL AWAY THE KEY SUPPORT AND THE WHOLE STRUCTURE WILL COLLAPSE.

"NOW IT IS TIME TO SEND OUT SCOUTS TO FIND OUT WHERE OUR ENEMIES ARE," SAYS VAL.
"IT IS NOT NECESSARY," ANSWERS GARM, "FOR I HAVE A THOUSAND SCOUTS AT WORK. LISTEN."

"IN THE DISTANCE YOU HEAR A CROW CALL. WERE IT A FIGHTING CALL OR A FOOD CALL OTHER CROWS WOULD ANSWER, BUT THAT WAS A DANGER CALL, A WARNING. SEE THE DOE AND HER FAWN? SHE IS ALERT BUT MOVING SLOWLY AWAY FROM A SOURCE OF DANGER. THERE ARE MORE SMALL BIRDS ABOUT THAN USUAL. THEY HAVE BEEN DISTURBED AT THEIR FEEDING."

TWO HOURS PASS, THEN A SENTINEL CROW SILENTLY TAKES ITS PERCH ON A TALL TREE. A FINE BUCK, ANTLERS BACK AND TAIL WAVING GOES LEAPING BY AND THE MAGPIES SET UP A CLAMOR. "IT IS TIME TO GO. OUR ENEMIES WILL BE HERE SHORTLY."

OLE RECEIVES THEIR WARNING WITH HEAVY SARCASM. "SO, YOU NEVER EVEN SAW THE RAIDERS, BUT YOU TELL ME THEY WILL BE HERE WITHIN THE HOUR. ARE YOU CHILDREN THAT YOU BELIEVE WHAT THE LITTLE BIRDIES AND BUTTERFLIES TELL YOU?"

"DON'T YOU WISH YOU HAD THE BRAINS OF A BUTTERFLY, OLE?" AND GARM POINTS ACROSS THE CLEARING WHERE THE RAIDERS ALREADY ARE GATHERING. OLE SLAMS AND BARS THE GATES. "OH, WOTAN," HE PRAYS, "MAKE ME AS WISE AS A BUTTERFLY!"

NEXT WEEK— **Bath Night**

10-25

1446

Our Story: FROM BEHIND THE STOUT PALISADE THAT GUARDS OLESON'S FARM PRINCE VALIANT WATCHES THE ENEMY PREPARE FOR THE ATTACK. TREES ARE FELLED AND STEPS NOTCHED IN THEM FOR SCALING THE WALLS. A HUGE LOG WILL SERVE AS A RAM.

WITH WILD YELLS THE ATTACK BEGINS, AND VAL SIGNALS THE TRUMPETER. SPEARS AND THROWING AXES FILL THE AIR AS THE MOB POURS INTO THE DRY RIVER BED IN FRONT OF THE DEFENSES.

FAR UP THE STREAM THEY HEAR THE TRUMPET'S CALL. THE DAM IS OPENED AND WITH A ROAR THE PENT-UP WATER FOAMS DOWN THE DRY BED.

IT IS NOT THAT THE RAIDERS OBJECT TO AN OCCASIONAL BATH, BUT THIS IS OVERDOING IT. IT IS DOUBTFUL IF ANY ONE OF THEM EVER WILL TAKE ANOTHER!

FOR A WHILE IT LOOKS AS IF VAL HAS CARRIED OUT HIS PLAN TOO WELL AND THE FARM BUILDINGS WILL BE WASHED AWAY, TOO, BUT THE PALISADE BREAKS THE FORCE OF THE FLOOD.

THE LOOT LEFT BEHIND BY THE RAIDERS IS CONSIDERABLE. THE GREAT AMOUNT OF WEAPONS GIVES VAL AN IDEA. IT IS SO DESPERATE, SO DANGEROUS THAT ITS VERY AUDACITY MAY BRING SUCCESS.

NEXT WEEK — **The Gadfly**

1447   11-1

Prince Valiant
IN THE DAYS OF KING ARTHUR
WRITTEN AND ILLUSTRATED BY HAROLD R FOSTER

Our Story: PRINCE VALIANT OPENED A DAM AND WASHED OUT A RAID. LEFT BEHIND IS THE LOOT OF MONTHS OF RAIDING AND ENOUGH WEAPONS FOR A HUNDRED MEN. WHEN THE SPOILS ARE DIVIDED OLE OLESON WILL BE WEALTHY FOR LIFE. VAL SETS OUT TO FIND HIMSELF AN ARMY.

SKOGUL ODERSON LEADS HIS FIERCE HOST NORTHWARD TOWARD VIKINGSHOLM, KING AGUAR'S STRONGHOLD, AND HE HAS ORDERED THAT NOTHING LIVING SHOULD SURVIVE THEIR PASSING.

AND THE ARMY IS BROKEN UP INTO GROUPS OF A HUNDRED OR MORE, FOR THIS IS A COUNTRY OF FARMS AND SMALL VILLAGES, AND SWORD AND FLAME COME TO THEM BEFORE THEY KNOW AN ENEMY IS NEAR.

KING AGUAR CALLS IN HIS CHIEFTAINS AND PREPARES FOR WAR. BUT WHERE? IT IS KNOWN THAT SKOGUL LANDED AN ARMY AT OSLOFJORD AND THEN VANISHED AMID THE HILLS AND FORESTS. EVEN THE KING'S SCOUTS CANNOT ESTIMATE THE NUMBER OR THE DIRECTION OF THE SCATTERED BANDS.

AND NEITHER DOES VAL. HE IS CONTENT TO SEEK THEM OUT ONE AT A TIME AND DESTROY THEM SOMEHOW. AND HE WILL NOT HAVE FAR TO SEEK, FOR A GROUP OF BOATS CAN BE SEEN IN THE DISTANCE, AND VAL, WHO HAS AS YET ONLY TWENTY MEN, SEEKS A DEFENSIVE POSITION.

"WHY IS THIS GREAT PILE OF LOGS HERE, GARM?" HE ASKS.
"THEY WILL BE ROLLED INTO THE STREAM WHEN THE WATER IS HIGH ENOUGH AND TAKEN TO THE VILLAGE WHERE, THIS WINTER, THEY WILL BE HEWN INTO BUILDING TIMBERS."

ACROSS THE RIVER A TREE IS FELLED, BLOCKING THE CHANNEL ON THAT SIDE.

1448   11-8

HAL FOSTER

THE WATER IS SWIFT HERE AND THE RAIDERS MUST HAUL THEIR BOATS UP. "I AM GREATLY TEMPTED TO TUMBLE THESE LOGS DOWN, GARM." "I WILL HELP YOU, MY PRINCE," ANSWERS GARM, TAKING UP HIS AXE.
NEXT WEEK—The Gadfly Stings Again

Prince Valiant
IN THE DAYS OF KING ARTHUR
WRITTEN AND ILLUSTRATED BY HAROLD R. FOSTER

Our Story: A BAND OF THE RAIDERS THAT ARE LAYING WASTE THE LAND OF THULE HAS CROSSED THE LAKE AND REACHED THE SWIFT WATER BELOW PRINCE VALIANT'S POSITION. THEY LOOK UP AS VAL SHOUTS TO HIS SCANTY FOLLOWERS TO TAKE THEIR POSITIONS.

THEN HE AND GARM DRIVE HOME THE WEDGES THAT WILL RELEASE THE STACKED LOGS.

AN AVALANCHE OF TIMBER ROARS DOWN THE SLOPE, DROWNING OUT THE SCREAMS OF TERROR FROM THE WAR BAND AS, HELPLESS, THEY AWAIT THEIR FATE.

MOST OF THE BOATS ARE CRUSHED UNDER THE LOGS, OTHERS CAPSIZED BY THE HUGE WAVE THEY CREATE. THOSE WHO SURVIVE FIND VAL'S ARCHERS AND SPEARMEN LINING THE SHORE. *AND THEY ARE SMILING!*

NO ATTENTION IS PAID TO THOSE WHO ESCAPE BY SWIMMING TO THE OPPOSITE SHORE. THEY ARE UNARMED, FOR HAD THEY RETAINED ARMS OR ARMOR OF ANY KIND, THEY WOULD HAVE DROWNED.

RUMORS SPREAD, EVEN IN THIS SPARSELY SETTLED LAND. TALES OF SKOGUL'S BANDITS, THEIR MYSTERIOUS APPEARANCES AND HORRIBLE DEEDS HAVE FILLED THE SETTLERS WITH FEAR. VAL FINDS MANY RECRUITS, BUT HE CHOOSES AND ARMS ONLY THE BEST.

1449   11-15

"TILL NOW WE HAVE BEEN AHEAD OF SKOGUL'S WAR BANDS AND COULD CHOOSE OUR OWN POSITION. NOW ONE BAND IS AHEAD OF US, FOR SEE, MY PRINCE, SOME LANDOWNERS' BUILDINGS HAVE BEEN PUT TO THE TORCH!"

NEXT WEEK– **Val Joins the Enemy**

Our Story: PRINCE VALIANT AND HIS BAND FIND THE SOURCE OF THE SMOKE AND FLAME THEY SAW THE EVENING BEFORE. THE FIERCE RUFFIANS OF SKOGUL'S INVADING ARMY HAVE BROUGHT FIRE AND DEATH TO A LARGE FARMSTEAD, AND VAL ALLOWS HIS HARDY TROOP PLENTY OF TIME TO VIEW THE HORRORS. LUCKY THE ONES WHO DIED FIGHTING; THE REST MUST HAVE WELCOMED DEATH AT THE LAST.

"THESE WERE YOUR OWN PEOPLE," SAYS VAL. "NEVER FORGET WHAT YOU SEE BEFORE YOU. WHEN WE FIND THE FIENDS WHO DID THIS DEED THESE VICTIMS MUST BE AVENGED!"

GARM PICKS UP THE TRAIL. "I SEE NO TRACKS OF HORSES, AND THE DEPTH OF THEIR FOOTPRINTS SHOWS THEY ARE WEIGHED DOWN WITH PLUNDER. WE SHOULD OVERTAKE THEM BY NIGHTFALL. THEY NUMBER OVER A HUNDRED."

BUT IT IS ONLY A FEW HOURS LATER THAT THEY WALK RIGHT INTO THE ENEMY. GARM, WHO IS LEADING, SIGNALS TO THOSE BEHIND HIM AND JOINS HIS FOES IN CUTTING TREES AND NOTCHING THEM TO MAKE SCALING LADDERS. NO ONE PAYS ANY ATTENTION TO THE NEW ADDITION TO SKOGUL'S FORCES.

VAL CHANGES TO LESS CONSPICUOUS COSTUME AND SCOUTS THE TARGET OF THE ATTACK, A COLLECTION OF HOUSES, BARNS AND CATTLE BYRES SURROUNDED BY A STRONG PALISADE. ALREADY THE HOUSE CARLS MAN THE WALLS, AND SERFS AND BONDSMEN ARE RUNNING IN FROM THE FIELDS.

1450

11-22

NOW THE RAIDERS LEAVE THE WOODS AND FORM IN LINE AT THE EDGE OF THE CLEARING, AND IN THE LAST ROW IS PRINCE VALIANT AND HIS BAND. THEN THE WAR DRUMS THUNDER AND THE SCREAMING HORDE RACES ACROSS THE OPEN GROUND.

NEXT WEEK – *The Mysterious Rearguard*

Prince Valiant
IN THE DAYS OF KING ARTHUR
WRITTEN AND ILLUSTRATED BY HAROLD R FOSTER

Our Story: THE DOUGHTY CHIEFTAIN BELLOWS DEFIANCE AT THE APPROACHING RAIDERS, AND HIS YOUNG HOUSE CARLS MAKE READY TO DEFEND THE PALISADE. THEN A STRANGE THING IS NOTICED. THE ADVANCING HORDE IS LEAVING A TRAIL OF VERY DEAD RUFFIANS BEHIND!

IN THE DIM FOREST PRINCE VALIANT'S MEN HAVE MINGLED WITH THE RAIDERS UNNOTICED, BUT WHEN THE ORDER IS GIVEN TO CHARGE ACROSS THE OPEN, VAL AND HIS BAND ARE IN THE LAST RANK. SILENTLY, EFFICIENTLY THEY SET ABOUT EVENING THE ODDS.

THE CHARGE HAS ALMOST REACHED THE PALISADE BEFORE THE TRICK IS DISCOVERED AND THE RAIDERS TURN ON VAL'S WAR BAND. THEN THE DEFENDERS HEAR A WELCOME CRY: "AGUAR! THULE! THULE! THULE!"

THE GATES SWING WIDE AND THE DEFENDERS SWARM OUT ECHOING THE WAR CRY. FOR A WHILE THE RAIDERS STAND FIRM, BUT FINDING THEMSELVES ATTACKED FROM BOTH FRONT AND REAR THEY FEEL A GROWING SENSE OF PANIC.

NO PRISONERS ARE TAKEN, FEW ESCAPE. FOR VAL'S MEN HAVE SEEN A SAMPLE OF THEIR SENSELESS BRUTALITY, AND THE LUST FOR REVENGE IS UPON THEM. BY SUNDOWN THE DEED IS DONE. THE SPOILS AND THE WOUNDED ARE BROUGHT INTO THE VILLAGE, AND THE BURIAL PARTY BEGINS ITS GRIM WORK.

1451   11-29-64

HAL FOSTER

IT IS TIME FOR SKOGUL ODERSON TO CALL HIS WAR BANDS TOGETHER FOR THE FINAL MARCH ON VIKINGSHOLM, BUT THREE OF THESE BANDS HAVE DISAPPEARED.

NEXT WEEK—**The Mysterious Monster**

Our Story: "WE HAVE MET AND DESTROYED THREE OF SKOGUL'S WAR BANDS. HE MUST HAVE LEARNED OF THIS BY NOW AND WILL MOST LIKELY SEND BACK A STRONG FORCE TO FIND THE CAUSE. GARM, SCOUT HIS POSITION AND LEARN WHAT YOU CAN."

SKOGUL HAS REACHED THE PLACE WHERE HIS WILD FOLLOWERS WERE TO RENDEZVOUS, BUT THERE IS NO TRACE OF HIS THREE MOST DESTRUCTIVE WAR BANDS.

GARM FOLLOWS SKOGUL'S TRAIL, WHICH LEADS UP THE RIVER VALLEY, THEN VEERS SHARPLY NORTHEAST INTO THE HILLS. THIS IS THE ROUTE BY WHICH SKOGUL COULD COME DOWN SUDDENLY UPON TRONDHEIM AND AN OPEN ROAD TO THE STRONGHOLD AT VIKINGSHOLM.

HE RETURNS SWIFTLY AND REPORTS TO PRINCE VALIANT: "SKOGUL HAS COMMITTED HIS ARMY TO ITS INTENDED ROUTE, AND WE CAN NOW SEND POSITIVE INFORMATION TO THE KING. HE IS ALSO SENDING A STRONG FORCE TO FIND OUT WHAT HAPPENED TO HIS MISSING WARRIORS."

THE FATE OF THE LOST WAR BANDS IS ALL TOO CLEAR. A FEARFUL MONSTER HAD COME OUT OF THE SOMBER FORESTS AND DEVOURED THEM. SOME OF THE CRUSHED AND TORN GEAR IS RECOGNIZED. IT IS A FRIGHTENING TALE SKOGUL'S MEN WILL TAKE BACK!

"GARM, YOU ARE TO STAY IN THE REAR AND REPORT ANY CHANGE IN THE ENEMY PLANS. NALL AND I WILL TAKE TWENTY MEN, CIRCLE THE ENEMY, AND HEAD FOR VIKINGSHOLM."

IT IS ROUGH TRAVELING THROUGH FORESTS AND OVER HILLS, BUT AT LAST THEY CIRCLE SKOGUL'S FORCES.

"NOW I MUST TRAVEL ALONE AND FAST. NALL, YOU AND YOUR MEN ARE TO LEAVE MONSTER FOOTPRINTS WHEREVER THEY WILL DO THE MOST GOOD.

NEXT WEEK - The Figurehead

1452   12-6-64

Prince Valiant
IN THE DAYS OF KING ARTHUR

WRITTEN AND ILLUSTRATED BY HAROLD R FOSTER

Our Story: PRINCE VALIANT BEGINS HIS LONG JOURNEY TO VIKINGSHOLM TO WARN THE KING OF THE APPROACH OF THE INVADING ARMY, AND NALL IS LEFT TO SPREAD FEAR IN THE APPROACHING HOST.

AND NALL HAS A GRIM SENSE OF HUMOR. A BEAR IS SLAIN, AND AFTER THEY TAKE WHAT MEAT THEY NEED, THE REST IS TORN INTO SHREDS, EVEN THE BONES CRUSHED AS IF THE MONSTER STOPPED FOR A LIGHT LUNCH.

AT A RIVER CROSSING NALL CREATES HIS MASTERPIECE. FOR THERE IN THE SOFT EARTH OF THE BANK IS EVIDENCE THAT THE MONSTER HAS LEAPED SEVENTY FEET!
SKOGUL HAD SCOURED THE BALTIC PORTS FOR RECRUITS, CHOOSING ONLY THE MOST BRUTAL......

.....WHO, LIKE MOST OF THEIR KIND, ARE SUPERSTITIOUS AND FEAR THE UNKNOWN. THEY ARE USED TO THE DANGERS OF THE SEA, BUT THESE SOMBER FORESTS WHERE MONSTERS DWELL FILL THEM WITH TERROR. THEY ARE CLOSE TO MUTINY, BUT SKOGUL DRAWS HIS SWORD AND CUTS DOWN THE RINGLEADERS.

NALL LEADS HIS SMALL BAND INTO TRONDHEIM TO WARN THE PEOPLE OF THE APPROACHING DANGER. IN THE SHIPYARDS HE SEES A DRAGON FIGUREHEAD BEING PREPARED FOR ONE OF THE LONGSHIPS. IT IS SO DELIGHTFULLY HIDEOUS THAT HE BORROWS IT.

1453

12-13-64

BESIDE THE TRAIL BY WHICH THE ENEMY MUST APPROACH THE TOWN HE SETS UP HIS 'MONSTER'.

NEXT WEEK— **The Berserker**

Our Story: NALL SETS UP THE FIGUREHEAD BESIDE THE TRAIL BY WHICH THE RAIDERS MUST COME, AND THEN SETTLES DOWN TO WAIT.

SKOGUL'S CONQUERING HORDE IS NOW BUT A FEAR-STRICKEN MOB AND AT SIGHT OF THE DRAGON GUARDING THE TRAIL, THEY HALT.

BUT WHEN THE DRAGON SLOWLY TURNS ITS HEAD TOWARD THEM, AND A TERRIBLE ROAR ECHOES THROUGH THE HILLS, THEIR TERROR IS MORE THAN THEIR FEAR OF THE CHIEFTAIN.

SKOKUL DOES NOT RUN. HIS TWISTED MIND IS FILLED WITH GREATER HORRORS. THE SLAVES WHO CARRY HIS PERSONAL THINGS CANNOT FLEE WITH THE REST; THEY ARE CHAINED.

HE ORDERS THESE SLAVES TO PREPARE A DRAUGHT FROM THE MYSTERIOUS SACRED MUSHROOMS AND DRAINS THE CUP. THE DRUG TAKES EFFECT AND HIS MADNESS BECOMES COMPLETE.

SKOGUL ODERSON HAS BECOME A BERSERKER AND MUST KILL ALL LIVING THINGS UNTIL HE HIMSELF IS KILLED. WOE TO MAN OR BEAST THAT IS IN HIS PATH!

12-20   1454

A SMALL BOY, DIPPING FOR SALMON FROM A FLIMSY SCAFFOLD, SEES HIM COMING, THE DRIPPING SWORD EVIDENCE OF HIS INTENT.

THE RUSHING RIVER COVERS THE HEAVILY-ARMED LEADER OF A CONQUERING HORDE, DEFEATED AT LAST BY A BOY ARMED ONLY WITH A NET AND A WET FISH.

NEXT WEEK — The War's End

Prince Valiant
IN THE DAYS OF KING ARTHUR

WRITTEN AND ILLUSTRATED BY HAROLD R FOSTER

Our Story: PRINCE VALIANT TROTS WEARILY INTO VIKINGSHOLM TO BRING WARNING OF AN INVADING ARMY, NOT KNOWING THAT THE ARMY IS NOW FLEEING IN TERROR AND THAT THEIR LEADER HAS MET HIS DOOM BY WAY OF A DEAD FISH.

IN SPITE OF HIS FAMILY'S ENERGETIC WELCOME, VAL IS ABLE TO BRING HIS MESSAGE TO HIS FATHER, THE KING.

THEN FROM THE MOUNTAIN TOPS THE SIGNAL FIRES GIVE THEIR WARNING. A COLUMN OF SMOKE BY DAY, A BLAZE AT NIGHT, AND THE HARDY SEAFARERS MAN THEIR LONGSHIPS AND BEAT TIME TO THE WAR SONGS WITH THEIR OARS.

FIRST TO ARRIVE IS BOLTAR, THE SEA KING. WHEN HE HEARS THAT SKOGUL'S ARMY AND FLEET OF SHIPS ARE TO MEET AND ATTACK VIKINGSHOLM BY BOTH LAND AND SEA HE IS MOST GENEROUS: "YOU, SIRE, CAN HAVE THE ARMY. MY BOYS AND I WILL TAKE CARE OF THEIR NAVY."

AND WHEN THAT NAVY SAILS INTO THE FJORD IT IS NOT SKOGUL'S ARMY THAT AWAITS THEM, BUT THAT OF KING AGUAR, AND RIGHT BEHIND THEM COME BOLTAR AND HIS 'BOYS'. AS THIS BECAME SOMETHING IN THE NATURE OF LIGHT EXERCISE RATHER THAN A BATTLE, IT IS NOT FURTHER RECORDED.

1455

12-27-64

HAL FOSTER

PRINCE ARN HAS TAKEN PART IN THE VICTORY ABOARD BOLTAR'S DRAGONSHIP, AND BOLTAR'S SON IS ALSO THERE. "HAVE YOU FORGOTTEN THE PROMISE YOUR MOTHER, THE SUN WOMAN, MADE TO MY PEOPLE?" HE ASKS.

NEXT WEEK— **The Oath**

IN '21, I DECIDED TO STICK WITH ART, BICYCLED 1000 MILES TO CHICAGO'S ART INSTITUTE. MY SERIOUS PAINTING RECEIVED THUNDEROUS APPLAUSE FROM ME, MILD APPROBATION FROM THE PUBLIC.

Above: Quiet (*oil on canvas, 1928*) *was painted by Foster the same year he illustrated the* Tarzan of the Apes *comic strip adaptation.*

Left: *Hal Foster spoofing his own short-lived fine art career.*

Opposite bottom left: *This photo of Foster from 1928 was taken at a Palette & Chisel Club outing in Fox River, Illinois, sixty miles northwest of Chicago. Although Foster is not listed as a member of the Palette & Chisel Club he appears in several photos with fellow Palenske-Young, Inc. employee F. William "Bill" Neuenfeldt.*

Opposite bottom right: *Foster's mastery of translucent watercolor painting.*

LAND AND SEA: HAL FOSTER'S FINE ART PAINTINGS

Compiled and annotated by Brian M. Kane

Quiet (opposite page) was painted by Hal Foster in 1928, which was the same year he adapted *Tarzan of the Apes* into a comic strip. Working for the Chicago-based Palenske-Young studio, Foster was a well-paid, mid-level advertising artist. Foster's advertisements appeared in prestigious magazines such as *McCall's* and *The Saturday Evening Post*, and he painted the National Parks for Union Pacific Railroad's major ad campaign (see *Prince Valiant, Vol. 7: 1949–1950*). Still, Foster craved the respect that came with being known as a Fine Artist, and had no desire to be a cartoonist.

As seen in the photograph below, *Quiet* was painted *en plein air*, or, simply, *outside*. It was a practice advocated by the 19th century Hudson River School, the Barbizon school, and the Impressionists. Foster certainly knew about these artists since his cover design for a 1928 issue of *The OilPull Magazine*

reproduced *The Gleaners* (1857) on the cover, and showcased a Foster painting on the back inspired, in part, by *The Sower* (1850); both by Jean-François Millet (see *Prince Valiant, Vol. 5: 1945–1946*). By the 1920s, when Foster began actively painting in oils, the prevailing movement in Fine Art landscape painting had shifted from American Realism to American Regionalism, but there is nothing *Modern* about Foster's style.

Much of Foster's initial formal art training was in Winnipeg, Manitoba, as a catalog artist working at Brigdens Limited under the art direction of Tom W. McLean. Before Brigdens, McLean worked at the Toronto-based design firm, Grip Limited, where he was friends with four of the founding members of *The Group of Seven*; an affiliation of landscape painters who were active from 1920–1933. While a case may be

made that *Quiet* can be thematically tied to paintings such as Tom Thomson's *Northern River* (1915), or A.Y. Jackson's *Frozen Lake, Early Spring, Algonquin Park* (1914), Foster was too much of a realist to wholly assimilate the abstractionist qualities of these artists.

However, Foster also studied at The Winnipeg School of Art under the guidance of renowned British watercolorist Alexander J. Musgrove, co-founder of the Manitoba Society of Artists. There are aspects of Musgrove's watercolor technique evident in Foster's work, especially in the way they both handled translucent colors, but it is Foster's oil painting of a farmstead on the following page that appears most heavily influenced by his teacher. Unfortunately, many of Foster's paintings are not dated (n.d.), but the signature on this painting is similar to some of his 1914–1917 wilderness cartoons, which

places it during the time he was studying under Musgrove.

Most of Foster's formulaic mountain oil paintings found in this gallery are small, and appear to have been painted during his time in Chicago; possibly for a class. Again, these are not named nor dated. What we do have are photos of Foster in three different homes throughout his lifetime (Evanston, IL; Redding, CT and Spring Hill, FL) that showcase his landscape paintings.

Although *Quiet* and some of his other paintings won awards at state fairs, Foster did not make a name for himself in the world of Fine Art. While *Quiet* is the most abstract of his oil paintings it is still heavily grounded in realism. Considering Foster's penchant for detail, it is doubtful he could have evolved into an artist such as Grant Wood, John Steuart Curry, or J. E. H. MacDonald. There is a certain irony in the realization that the Fine Art world became too Modernist for an artist who made a name for himself illustrating all things Mediæval.

The maritime painting *Running before the Wind* at the top of page 8 was provided by Andrew Murray Fine Art (murriarti.com).

Special thanks to Geoffrey K. Mawby for permitting access to the painting *Quiet*, and Alan Geho of Ralphoto Studio for photographing some of these paintings. The maritime painting *Running before the Wind* at the top of page #127 appears courtesy of Andrew Murray Fine Art (murriarti.com).

Opposite Top: This oil on board landscape appears to have been painted while Foster was still living in Winnipeg, and shows a strong influence from one of his teachers, Alexander J. Musgrove.

Opposite Below and Right: Two more undated Foster oil landscapes on canvas.

Several of the oil paintings on these two pages appear to be experiments in learning the technique of oil painting.

Below: *Hal Foster in his Redding, Connecticut studio. Note the oil landscape on the wall behind him.*

Above: Untitled *(gouache on illustration board, 1916)*.

Below: French Fishing Boats *(gouache on illustration board, 1916)*.

Above: Running before the Wind *(watercolor)*.

Below: Untitled *(gouache on illustration board, 1916)*.

Above: *Ribbons from the 1936 Kansas Free Fair, Foster won for his art. Featured are* Quiet *(page 120),* Shylock *(see Prince Valiant, Vol. 4: 1943-1944),* Merchants of Bagdad *(sic, top right), and* Marine Phantasy *(sic, right).*

Below left: *The evolution of Foster's signature.*

Below right: *Helen and Hal Foster in their Spring Hill, Florida home with some of the paintings from this gallery hanging on the wall.*

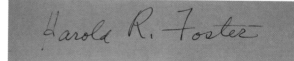

IN OUR NEXT VOLUME:

PRINCE VALIANT

VOL. 15: 1965-1966

Val's son, Prince Arn leads an expedition to the New World where trade deals soon turn into hostage negotiations. When enemy tribes attack, Arn's band of Vikings team up with the Algonquins to repel the invaders, leading to the discovery of the St. Lawrence seaway. Val recovers the Singing Sword, Aleta has mermaid encounters, and Mordred plans to attack Val's family when they are at their most vulnerable.